BLOODLUST BY MIDNIGHT

Last Witch Standing, Book 2

DEANNA CHASE

Bayou Moon Press, LLC

About This Book

Being a badass witch isn't always what it's cracked up to be. Vampire Hunter Phoebe Kilsen's world is falling apart. Her shifter partner has been drugged and is in danger of turning rabid, and her brother has disappeared into thin air... literally.

Just as Phoebe is on the verge of making a major breakthrough on finding her long-lost brother, a new drug is introduced into New Orleans's black market. It's Phoebe's job to find out who is responsible and neutralize them before New Orleans is overrun with rabid wolves. With Eadric Allcot as her number one suspect, she finds herself once again facing down the most powerful vampire in New Orleans. But when her partner Dax is viscously attacked with the drug, she needs Allcot's help to save him. Now she's forced to make a choice between defying orders and saving the one she loves. The decision is an easy one for Phoebe. She's willing to break all the rules to save Dax... and if luck is on her side, she might even find her brother.

Chapter One

Faint, almost undetectable footsteps echoed behind me in the still night air. If it hadn't been for my newly spelled silver pendant that amplified noise, it'd be impossible to hear him. The vampire must've thought himself clever, patiently tracking me from the moment I stepped out of my car, waiting for just the right moment to get the jump on me. As if I, Phoebe Kilsen, a witch and vampire hunter for the Void, would ever be so careless.

I held back a scoff as I entered the gardens that led to New Orleans's oldest library. Oak trees lined the path, and heavy storm clouds blocked out the full moon. The early-summer humidity was so thick and oppressive that sweat rolled down my spine. After the shit day I'd had, all I wanted was a beer and a shower. And that was exactly what was waiting for me after I met with the swamp witch, Simone. She had a file full of research just waiting for me in the library. But first it appeared I needed to hand the stalker vamp his ass.

Clutching my phone with one hand, I pretended to check

a message as I grabbed the hilt of my silver dagger and slowed my pace. His footsteps quickened.

Good. *I'm waiting, asshole.*

After finding out another shifter had died of a suspicious drug overdose earlier that day, I was more than ready to take out my frustration on someone who deserved it. I could still see the radiant smile and sparkling blue eyes of the young barista who worked at my corner coffee shop. Her name was Rhea, and I'd gotten to know her a little bit after she started dating Leo, the young shifter my partner Dax had sort of taken under his wing.

The pair had been sweet, completely head over heels for each other, and if I was honest, a little nauseating to witness. But even as cynical as I could sometimes be about romantic relationships, I'd been happy for them. Young love was always just so… hopeful.

But then I'd been the one to find Rhea this morning in that back alley on vampire row, a needle jammed in her arm, her lips blue and her eyes lifeless. I hadn't even suspected that she'd been a drug user.

"Fuck," I muttered, trying and failing to erase her image from my mind.

The vampire's sinister chuckle was a mere whisper in my ear, indicating he was right behind me.

I spun, aiming my light-filled dagger straight for his chest. It was no surprise when he easily blocked my blow, but I was ready for him, my knee already connecting with his groin.

"You bitch," he snarled, holding his crotch with one hand and reaching for my neck with the other.

I danced backward out of his reach. "Why are you following me, Tanner?"

The moment the vamp had stumbled into the light from

the nearby lamppost, I'd recognized him. He was tall and thin with beady eyes that made him resemble a weasel. And because that description also applied to his ambiguous morality, he was perfect for Allcot's gang of henchmen.

He took a step closer, his thin lips curving into a sinister smile as he scanned me from head to toe.

"Take a good look, jackass," I said, "because your eyes are about the only thing you'll ever get to lay on me." It was obvious that he was imagining sinking his fangs into my neck. But we both knew that if he tried that, I wouldn't hesitate. He'd be ash in seconds.

"Christ, Kilsen. You've sure got a stick up your ass tonight. What's the problem? Does that shifter of yours need lessons on how to keep you satisfied?" He jerked his hips forward and leered at my modest cleavage peeking out from my V-neck T-shirt.

I gave him a flat stare.

His grin widened. "I've got some instructional videos. I'll lend them to your boy, Marrok. I'm sure it's better for everyone when you're not so… tense."

Without a second thought, I let my dagger fly and was rewarded when the vampire dodged to the right, in the exact same direction I'd aimed my weapon. The vampire froze as the blade lodged in his chest, just to the left of his heart.

I leaped forward, grabbing his neck with one hand. "How's this for tense?" I spun him around and slammed his back into the lamppost just because I could.

Tanner reached for the knife, no doubt desperate to get it out of his chest, but I beat him to it, wrapping my free hand around the hilt.

"That's what you get for spewing lewd comments about my relationship with Dax. Make one more move, and I'll end you. All it will take is one twist of this blade and your heart will be shredded. Got it?"

He gulped, then nodded.

"Now, why are you following me?" I asked through clenched teeth, more than ready to be done with Allcot's flunky. "Does your boss want something?"

He averted his gaze and shook his head.

"You're lying." I tightened my grip around his neck. None of Allcot's people did anything without his approval. If one of his vampires was following me, the city's most notorious vampire hunter, he'd ordered it. "What does he want?"

"Nothing," Tanner spat out, his voice barely audible from the force of my hold.

I didn't have the time or patience for this. And honestly, I didn't give a shit what Allcot wanted. He was a selfish bastard who was only on your side when it suited his purposes. There were only two things I cared about in that moment: who was supplying the street drugs that were taking down the werewolf community and how to find my missing brother. I was already well aware Allcot either couldn't or *wouldn't* answer either question. So whatever he wanted was of no concern to me. And I was done playing with Tanner.

But instead of using the dagger to end him as I'd threatened, I let go of the hilt and raised my wrist, exposing my magical sun agate I'd set into a leather wristband. Then I said, "*Siste.*"

The brilliant white light that mimicked sunlight flared from the stone, instantly knocking the vampire out. He slid to the pavement, eyes rolled to the back of his head. His knees hit the ground, and he started to career forward. I quickly reached for him, catching him before he fell flat onto my dagger. Killing him wasn't in the plan. Not one of Allcot's vamps. Taking out one of his without due cause would mean war.

I laid him out on the sidewalk, pulled out my phone, and called the office. My handler picked up on the first ring.

"What do you need?" Zena asked.

"Transport crew. I've got a downed vamp. Knocked out, minor knife wound to the chest." I rattled off the location and crouched near the vamp.

"They're on their way," Zena confirmed. Then she added, "I see it's been a long day for you. Try to stay out of trouble for the rest of the evening, huh?"

I let out a humorless laugh. "I was headed to the library, Zena. Blame this one on Allcot. I don't know what he's up to, but I'm in no mood for his bullshit. Once they get his goon back to the Void, it's up to the director what she wants to do with him."

Zena let out a low whistle. "Allcot again. He's a piece of work."

"You're telling me. I'll be in tomorrow morning to do the paperwork," I said. "Tell Director Halston I've gone home for the night."

"Is that where you're going?" Zena asked, her tone skeptical.

"Nope."

She chuckled. "I didn't think so."

After we ended the call, I yanked my dagger out of Tanner's chest. The wound was deep, but being that he was a vampire, there was very little blood. Good. That meant he hadn't fed recently. Normally the wound would heal fairly quickly, but because my blade was tinged with ancient magic from my bloodline, this one would linger. A small, satisfied smile claimed my lips. One would think the vampires of New

Orleans would learn. It was rare for a vamp to mess with me without earning a souvenir.

Of course, this one had been sent by Allcot, the bastard. Just last month I'd helped him save his consort, Pandora, from certain death. You'd think that would earn me some good will from the notorious vampire. Apparently not. That was no surprise, really. Eadric Allcot, the owner of Cryrique, the most powerful vampire organization in the southern half of the country, was a ruthless bastard. He did what he wanted, when he wanted, to whomever he wanted. Loyalty only went so far. I just wondered what the hell he wanted from me.

On any other day, I'd just show up at his compound and demand answers. But that night, I needed answers from someone else.

The moment the transport crew arrived, I waved and took off at a dead run for the library. I had an appointment to keep. After a month of searching, I was finally going to get some answers about my brother's disappearance.

Exactly four weeks ago, I'd watched my brother disappear into thin air. He'd been there one minute and was gone the next. Witches could wield spells and do some amazing things, but disappearing into thin air? That was impossible. Or at least I'd thought so until I'd witnessed it with my own two eyes.

For weeks I'd searched archived records at the Void and had put the call out for experts in vanishing spells. I'd come up completely empty. Everyone said it was impossible. Magic just didn't work that way. But then two days ago, I'd gotten a call from a swamp witch who said she had the information I'd been looking for. But she hadn't been willing to say anything over the phone. She said she'd be in touch on where to meet.

An hour later, a messenger had shown up with a note. The only thing the note had contained was the location, the date, and the time.

After running a thorough background check on the witch, I was certain she was the real deal. Her reputation, while eccentric, was legendary. She was in her late seventies, and her strength and knowledge were unparalleled. I hadn't been able to find one person who'd met or heard of her who wasn't in awe of her.

If anyone could help me find my brother, Simone Bernard was the one. The library, an old Victorian structure, was all but hidden in the shadows. Only one light shone from the second floor, acting as a beacon. I took the porch stairs two at a time and rushed inside. Candlelight illuminated the book-filled shelves lining the foyer.

"Simone?" I called out, slowing my pace, listening for the witch. The library was a private collection owned by the Arcane—the government paranormal investigation agency I worked for. The Arcane oversaw all paranormal activity. I worked for the Void division, the undercover branch that moved in the shadows.

I'd been to the library before, but since most, if not all, of the records the library held had been scanned into the computers and housed at the office, it wasn't a place I frequented on a regular basis.

Simone didn't answer. Hadn't she said to meet her in the front parlor? I quickly slipped into the room to the right and scanned the darkened space. There was a couch and two club chairs in the middle with books lining the walls. No Simone.

If she'd already left, Tanner was going to wish he'd never crossed my path. Deep in my gut, I knew time wasn't on my side. The longer my brother Seth was missing, the harder it was going to be to find him. We'd already spent eight years apart before he'd suddenly shown up in New Orleans last month. I wasn't going to spend the next eight wondering what had happened to him.

Remembering the light in the second-floor window, I headed up the stairs. The soft candlelight flickered from a room at the end of the hall, and I followed it like a moth to a flame.

"Simone?" I called again just before I reached the doorway. The sticky presence of magic in the air made my skin tingle, alerting me to the presence of another witch. The tension drained out of my shoulders. The magic was so strong—she had to be in there.

No answer.

I quickly scanned the room, seeing no one. But still the magic lingered. I moved into the room and as I passed a large wooden desk, I spotted her. She was lying on the ground, blood trickling from her neck.

"Son of a— Goddamn it!" Rushing to her side, the first thing I noticed was the savage bite on her neck. "Vampire," I whispered. There was no doubt. The two puncture wounds told me everything I needed to know. I automatically reached for her wrist to check her pulse. And that's when I saw the neon-green syringe clutched in her hand.

It was the same unusual type of syringe that had been attached to the needle stuck in Rhea's arm that morning.

Chapter Two

"Forget the vamp," I gasped out, still out of breath from running down the stairs and out the front door of the library with Simone's limp body in my arms. "She's alive, but she needs blood. Now!"

The two medics from the transport team looked up from the gurney they were already rolling toward the van. Tanner was strapped down and still knocked out. If they'd done their job correctly, he was in no danger of going anywhere even if he woke from my spell.

"Jesus," Finn said as he rushed to my side and focused on the gash in her neck. He glanced back at Tanner. "Did that vamp do this?"

"I don't know." Had he? "I don't think so. Tanner was following me into the gardens. But he could've been the distraction while one of Allcot's other vampires attacked her."

"I've got to get her to the van. I can start a transfusion in there on the way back to the Void." Finn took Simone from my arms and rushed her out of the garden.

I watched him leave, then turned my attention to Tanner, who was still passed out on the gurney. "Did you check his pockets?"

Victoria nodded. "We didn't find anything too unusual. There's an evidence bag at his feet."

I grabbed the clear plastic bag while the other witch continued to roll Tanner out of the gates and onto the brick sidewalk.

"We did find a couple of condoms though." She shook her head, looking disgusted. "The only reason vamps keep those on them is if they refuse to disclose their vamp status."

"Jackass." I had no trouble believing Tanner would pretend to be something he wasn't. Vampires didn't carry disease, and they couldn't get anyone pregnant. If he was wearing a condom, it was only because he didn't want his partner to know he had fangs. And if a vamp had just fed, his partner wouldn't have any reason to believe he was anything other than human. Fresh blood warmed a vampire right up and gave him a rosy glow. Shaking my head, I studied the contents of the evidence bag. Other than the condoms, there wasn't anything unusual… or was there? I took a closer look, then pointed to a small container that at first glance looked like a mint tin. "Is this what I think it is?"

She nodded. "It has traces of red powder. We still need to test it, but I'm pretty sure it's that new street drug. Scarlet is what they're calling it."

It was the same drug that had killed Rhea. I knew it well. It was an extra-potent drug that was a manufactured mirror of opium and strong enough that it worked on vampires and shifters. If humans took it, the dose was often fatal. Our bodies just couldn't handle it. "You need to run a tox screen on Simone as soon as possible. If this is in her system—" I pulled the syringe that she'd been clutching out of my pocket and showed it to Victoria. "She was holding this."

"Shit!" Victoria took off at a dead run.

I glanced once at Tanner, who was still passed out, and sprinted after her. Finn already had Simone in the van. Victoria jumped in and said, "She needs a Scarlet detox shot now!"

Finn's lips pressed into a thin line as he immediately rummaged in his emergency bag and pulled out a syringe. Without another word, he jabbed the needle into Simone's chest.

The witch's eyes flew open as she sucked in a gasp of air. In the next moment, Simone's eyes rolled into the back of her head and she went limp.

"Whoa. What the hell was that?" I asked, climbing into the van to get a better look.

"Special antidote. If she's been drugged with Scarlet, there was no time to do a tox screen or administer an IV." Victoria whipped out a stethoscope and listened carefully to Simone's heart. She closed her eyes, and after a moment she nodded. "Heart rate is up, but that's to be expected. Let's get her out of here. She needs a full workup."

Finn checked her pupils, noted her pulse rate, then turned to me. "Did you see her take the drug?"

I shook my head. "No." I produced the green syringe, handing it to him. "It's empty, but I've only seen this type of green syringe once before. This morning. A young shifter had one stuck in her arm. It was a Scarlet overdose."

Both of the Void employees stared at me, their eyes asking the question neither of them wanted to voice.

"I found her too late."

Victoria nodded and held out an evidence bag to Finn.

He dropped the syringe inside, and as I watched them work, I had an overwhelming urge to wash my hands… or take a scalding-hot shower. I didn't want to be anywhere near that drug. It was extremely dangerous to anyone who wasn't immortal.

I hopped out of the van. "I'll get Tanner."

"Leave him," Finn said, reaching to close one of the back doors. "I already have backup on the way."

"I'll stay." I was unwilling to leave an unconscious vampire out on the street. There was no telling what could happen if he woke up. Or worse, if some clueless do-gooder stumbled upon him.

"Suit yourself. See you back at the office." The other door slammed shut and the van took off, its lights flashing as the sirens rang in my ears.

I walked back over to Tanner, glanced down at his beady-eyed face, and felt my gut churn. The green syringes weren't just a coincidence. I was sure of it. And that meant there was some sort of a connection between Rhea's overdose and Simone's attack. I prayed Simone would be awake and have some information when I got back to the Void. Because whoever was responsible for this… I was going to make them pay.

I sat next to Tanner's cell, drumming my fingernails on the small portable table. The vampire was awake, but he was lying down, staring at the ceiling, pretending he hadn't noticed me. I knew better. He was grinding his teeth to the beat of my drumming.

"The sooner you tell me why you attacked Simone, the

sooner we can end this torture," I said, eyeing the pouch of blood the guard had brought for him. I'd confiscated it, refusing to let him feed until he answered my questions.

Nothing. No reaction.

I made a notation of the time and his nonresponse just as I had each time I'd asked over the past two hours. He was consistent at least. Always silent, no denials. "When's the last time you fed?" I glanced at the clock on the wall. "Twelve hours?" That was how long it'd been since I found Simone.

Still no response, but he did glance over at the clock, then at the pouch of blood sitting on the floor next to me.

"Hungry?" I asked.

His eyes darted to the pouch again. Then he growled.

"Just answer my questions and I'll let you feed."

"Kilsen," a familiar, angry voice said from behind me.

Dammit. I stood and turned my attention to Eadric Allcot. He was dressed in an expensive suit, his blond hair slicked back. He'd been turned in his late teens, but despite his young appearance, he exuded power and had an arrogance that only the powerful seemed to possess. The vampire towered over me, his angular jaw clenched as he glared at me.

"Eadric," I said, unfazed by his presence. "What can I do for you this morning?"

"You can let my employee out of that cage." His eyes flickered to the blood pouch. His expression turned darker. "Since when is it acceptable to attack a vampire without provocation?"

"Oh, I was provoked." I crossed my arms over my chest and stared him in the eye, noting his gray eyes had almost turned black with anger. He wasn't wearing the colored contacts he'd become so fond of recently. Good. It made it easier to read his mood. "You can bet on that. Next time you want me for something, why don't you try a phone call?"

His brow wrinkled for just a moment before it smoothed out and his expression turned blank. "I didn't send Tanner to find you."

"Then why was he stalking me?" I asked, casting a glance at the incarcerated vampire.

"I wasn't stalking you," Tanner said with a sneer as he rubbed the hole in his chest. "Why would anyone stalk a crazy bitch like you?"

My fingers curled into fists. "You tell me, Tanner. Why was it I could feel your stale-ass breath on my neck right before I jammed my knee in your balls?"

Allcot cocked an eyebrow in his flunky's direction.

Tanner raised both hands and shrugged. "I was just bored and fucking around. She's the one who attacked me. I never laid a finger on her."

I opened my mouth to protest but closed it when the director suddenly slipped through the door, her eyes narrowed and her lips pressed into a thin line. What was Director Halston doing down in the basement?

"Kilsen, let the vampire go," she ordered, her blue fae wings fluttering in agitation.

"But—"

"He's right," she barked, cutting me off. The small fae was barely five feet tall, but her confidence and take-charge demeanor always seemed to fill the room. "It says right here in the report you signed that the vampire in question never even touched you before you buried your knife in his chest. You're lucky you don't have a lawsuit on your hands."

"I never said I wouldn't sue." Tanner was on his feet, a gleam shining in his dark eyes. He raked his gaze over me again and added in a disturbingly seductive voice, "But if you want to settle, I'm open to negotiations."

His words made my skin crawl. The problem with vamps like him was that it was all fun and games until it wasn't. All too often their "fun" turned into assault. And while I could certainly handle him on any given day, most of the women walking the streets of New Orleans weren't Void-trained witches who could bring a vamp to his knees with just one spell. "If I ever hear you speaking to me or anyone else like that again, you're going to have much bigger problems than a hole in your chest, got it?" I said, letting my gaze linger on his crotch.

His gaze followed mine, and he growled as he took a step back as if I'd already cursed him.

"That's enough," Allcot said. "Tanner, you aren't going to sue Kilsen, and she isn't going to curse your dick." The head of Cryrique glanced over at me. "And *you* aren't going to go around stabbing my people either. Otherwise, you and I are going to have a problem. Got it?"

I scowled at him. "Just keep your people away from me. I don't appreciate being harassed while I'm doing my job."

"Understood." Allcot nodded at the door to the cell. "Now release my employee before I get impatient."

Arrogant Jackass. What was he even doing there? Bailing a minion out of jail wasn't usually on Allcot's personal to-do list. There were others he usually sent in his place. I glanced between them, trying to work out what made Tanner so special. Last I knew, he was just a vampire who worked security at the Red Door, Allcot's nightclub over in vampire territory.

Director Halston let out an impatient sigh. "Kilsen, release the vampire."

I gritted my teeth and punched the code into the security panel. The buzzer went off and the door slid open. Tanner stalked out of the cell, grabbed the blood pouch at my feet, and tore into it.

Allcot waited patiently for his employee to finish his breakfast, then told him, "Kilsen is off-limits. Get in her way again and I'll leave you here."

Without another word, the pair strode out the door and up the stairs. I turned to the director. "What the hell was that about? That vampire is a suspect in the attack on Simone."

She shoved her hands into the pockets of her white lab coat. "How so? He obviously hadn't fed recently. And thanks to your overzealous attack, we don't have anything else that will stick either. Reread the report, Kilsen. Tell me where it says the vampire attacked you. Or even threatened to attack you."

I didn't need to. She was right. Tanner had pissed me off by invading my personal space and being a general jackass, but he hadn't actually touched me. I'd made the first move. And even then, all he'd done was defend himself. "Shit," I muttered, running a hand through my long dark hair. "You're right. But we both know he was up to something. Allcot's vampires know better than to mess with me."

"If they didn't before, they sure as hell do now," she said, already striding out of the room. "Clean yourself up and meet me in my office in ten minutes."

I glanced down at my bloodstained T-shirt and grimaced. It had to be from when I'd carried Simone. I'd been at the Void all night doing paperwork, checking on Simone, and interrogating Tanner, and I hadn't even noticed.

The sound of the clock ticking in the silent room drew my attention. It was just past nine. And well past the time Dax would've shown up at my house to pick me up for work. I took the stairs two at a time and ran into the locker room. I wasted no time stripping and jumping into the shower. Five minutes later, my hair still dripping, I pulled clean clothes from my locker and glanced at my phone. Eight texts, two messages, and five missed phone calls.

"Shit," I muttered. Willow and Dax were losing their minds because I hadn't come home the night before and hadn't answered either of their calls. After pulling on fresh jeans and a plain black tee, I texted both of them, letting them know I was at the office.

Dax texted back immediately. *Your brother has been sighted.*

Chapter Three

_M_y heart stopped, then got lodged in my throat as I typed back. _Where?_

I stared at my phone, clutching the device so tightly I was sure my hand would cramp. No response.

Dax?

Nothing. Too impatient to wait, I pulled up his name and hit Call. It went straight to voice mail. "You've got to be kidding me," I said into the phone. "You can't just text me that Seth has been sighted and then nothing. Call me back ASAP."

After I ended the call, I checked my text messages again and scowled at the lack of response. "Dax had better be either incapacitated or beating the shit out of some rogue vampire. Otherwise, I'm going to kick his ass."

"It must suck to be your partner," a woman with short red hair said as she glided into the dressing area. The witch was a new tracker who'd just started with the Void a few months ago. "What are you going to do next? Stab him in the chest? I never thought the badass Phoebe Kilsen would let some two-bit bouncer get under her skin."

I scowled at her but said nothing, unwilling to take her bait. There was no doubt my fuckup with Tanner was flying through the gossip mill like wildfire.

"Watch it," Sabastian, the witch's partner, said from behind her. "Kilsen has been in rare form lately. You don't want to fuck with her." The tall, wide-shouldered shifter winked at me as he handed the witch a file. "Besides, you don't want to get on the bad side of the witch who has the highest vampire-takedown rate in the entire organization."

"She what?" The witch turned to stare at me, her mouth open.

I gave her a tight smile, nodded at Sabastian, and then took off. Who cared about my record? I hadn't gotten to Simone soon enough, and she was still lying unconscious in one of the med units. Meanwhile, someone had spotted my missing brother. Records didn't mean shit to me.

The fluorescent lights flickered in the stark white halls of the Void building as I hurried upstairs to Halston's office.

"You're late," the director barked from where she stood behind her desk. Her frizzy gray hair was pulled back, and she was wearing black-rimmed glasses as she studied a file.

"My apologies. I was—"

"Never mind." She waved a hand. "Sit down."

"I'll stand."

She pierced me with her dark eyes. "You're agitated."

I shrugged one shoulder. "I don't trust Allcot. A young shifter, who I'm not at all convinced was a drug addict, died of an overdose, and a powerful swamp witch was attacked while waiting for me in the Arcane library. I don't know how it all adds up, but my gut says it's all connected. And we just let Allcot take one of his vamps out of here without answering any questions. So yeah, I'm agitated."

"Good. Because I think you're right. Something is fishy, and it looks like Cryrique is right in the middle of it." She passed me the very thin file. "Here's a list of shifters who've suffered drug overdoses in the past two weeks. Five barely survived. The other three have perished. I want you and Marrok to follow up on all of them. Find out who their dealers are, if they were regular users, and any other relevant details of their lives. If I'm correct about my suspicions, then someone is using a modified and deadly version of Scarlet to deliberately try to purge this city of shifters."

I glanced at the file. There were eight victims listed. Rhea's name was at the bottom. I sucked in a sharp breath. If someone had deliberately killed Rhea, I was going to produce their head on a silver platter. "By somebody, do you mean Allcot?"

"Maybe. It's hard to say. Just follow the leads and report back to me." She pulled out her chair and sat at the desk as she punched a few keys on her computer. "Fill in Marrok when he finally deigns to grace us with his presence. If Allcot or any of his employees are involved, do not make a move before you inform me. Understood?"

"Understood."

She gave me a short nod as she picked up her phone and instructed her assistant to get a director from another branch on the line. She glanced up and jerked her head toward the door. I'd been dismissed.

"Dax?" I banged on the door of his new place in the Irish

Channel neighborhood. He'd recently moved into one half of a shotgun double that was walking distance from the home I shared with Willow and Talisen.

There was no answer.

I pulled out my phone and texted him again. He hadn't answered me since he'd dropped the bomb that Seth had been spotted. That had been forty-five minutes earlier. If the man wasn't trapped under something heavy, I was going to kick his ass.

"He left early this morning." The neighbor had come out onto her porch. She was wearing bright orange hot pants, a formfitting tank top, and had a cigarette dangling from her perfectly painted pink fingernails. "I was just getting in from work when he ran out the door. Looked like he was in a hurry."

"Thanks," I said, giving her a nod. "Did you see Leo? The blond kid who's been crashing on his couch?"

She shook her head as she took a long drag of her cigarette. A lock of her curly black hair fell into her eyes and she brushed it back. "Nope. Last I saw him, he was sittin' on this porch drinking a twelve-pack of Abita. He looked rough. I tried to cheer him up. Offered him free passes to the midnight burlesque show where I work, but he said he wasn't up to it." She took another drag of her cigarette and gave me a half shrug. "First time I've ever had a man turn down free passes."

"There was a…" I shook my head. "We lost someone important to him last night. Don't take it personally."

Her face fell, and sympathy exuded from her as she stepped forward and placed a hand on my arm. A faint trace of unwieldy magic skittered over my skin, and I jerked back out of reflex.

"Sorry," she said, obviously annoyed as she held her hands up. "Didn't mean to invade your personal space. Christ," she muttered as she turned back to her door. "That's what I get for trying to show some empathy. Everyone's so touchy these days."

"Wait," I called, still unsettled. Her power had felt wild, uncontrolled, just the way my own had when it had manifested in my teen years. Did she know she had magic? Had she felt mine when she'd placed her hand on me?

The woman paused just before she stepped into her house. "What?"

"What's your name?"

"Iris. Yours?"

"Phoebe." I shoved my hands in my pockets as I cleared my throat, not quite sure how to broach the subject. But I quickly became impatient with myself. I usually wasn't one to mince words. "Do you know you're a witch?"

"Um... what?" She chuckled softly. "Are you sure you haven't been drinking this morning? You look a little... Well, let's just say that you look a lot like me and my girlfriends after a particularly fun night out on the town."

I took a step closer and shook my head. "No, I haven't been drinking, unfortunately. I was working. It was a long night."

"I can relate," she said with a small smile. "New Orleans is that kind of town."

"It's also one full of the supernatural," I pressed. "Vampires, shifters, and yes, witches like you and me."

She stared at me, her brow crinkled, then she shook her head. "Listen, I don't know why you're so fixated on—"

I reached out and placed my hand on her arm. Magic pulsed at my fingertips, calling hers to the surface.

23

"Whoa!" She jerked her arm back. "What the hell were you doing?"

"Calling your magic," I said as I reached into my pocket and pulled out a tattered business card. All it had was my name and a phone number on it. "If you want to learn about your gift, you can reach me at this number."

Iris's hand shook a little as she took the card. "I... That's not..." She glanced up at me, her expression full of confusion. "I can't be a witch."

"You can," I said. "And you are. You have two choices: bury it and hope it doesn't come back to bite you in the ass or learn how to control it and open up a whole new world of opportunities."

She was still standing on the porch, staring at the card as I jumped in my car and headed back to the Arcane library.

Chapter Four

*D*ax strode down the dank alley, fuming. The kid he'd opened his home to had not only taken a swing at him, he'd broken Dax's goddamn phone as well. Then Leo had stormed out, vowing to rip the throat out of whoever was responsible for Rhea's death.

Dax's first instinct was to let the kid cool off. Unfortunately, the only people Rhea could've gotten Scarlet from was the city's vampire or shifter population. And if Leo picked a fight with the wrong one, the kid would be the next one in the city morgue. So instead of heading into the office and working on whatever new case the director had for him and Phoebe, he was working his way down Basin Street, tracking down Leo.

Over a hundred years ago, Basin Street had been the center of Storyville, the red-light district where brothels had flourished. So had jazz clubs and any other sinful establishment anyone could think up. But after the area was closed down in the early nineteen hundreds, all those establishments had gone underground. A few years ago,

Allcot and his investors decided to bring Storyville back. Only instead of brothels, they opened blood banks, aka feeding houses, and supernatural nightclubs just for the paranormal community. It was where one went when they were tracking down a vamp or shifter who liked to party.

Of course, since it was just after nine in the morning, most of the establishments were currently closed. It was hard to cater to vampires during the day when most would combust in the sunlight. There were some who were daywalkers, thanks to Willow Rhoswen and her unusual gift of being able to turn vamps into sun-resistant creatures, but not enough to justify businesses staying open during the day.

That meant if Leo was still around, there were only two places he could be. Howlers or the Swamp. Dax headed for the Swamp. It was the type of place that welcomed all kinds of supernaturals. It was also the kind of place where an arrogant young kid would get his ass kicked if he wasn't careful.

The stench of overflowing garbage with a whiff of rotten oranges assaulted his senses, making him fight his gag reflex. He ground his teeth and quickened his pace.

"Damn kid," Dax muttered, barely able to control his frustration. Rhea's death had been a blow to all of them. He knew Leo was in pain, but running out and getting himself killed wasn't going to solve anything.

He strode into the Swamp, pausing for just a moment to let his eyes adjust. "Paradise City" by Guns N' Roses blared from the sound system. The stench of stale blood filled the air, leaving no question that the club was also a feeding ground for vamps.

"Hey, handsome," a sickly-sweet female voice said as a woman slipped her arm through his.

Dax glanced down at her pale, thin face and tried not to let his revulsion show. There were purple smudges beneath her eyes and unhealed vampire bites on her neck.

Classic feeder.

"I'm looking for someone," he said, extracting himself from her grip.

"Well, looks like you found her. I'm Lexi. And you are?" She put her hand on his back and slid it down to cup his ass.

"Dax. Now remove your hand or I'll do it for you," he said through clenched teeth.

"Touchy." She shrugged and swept a cold, calculating gaze down his body. "I guess that means you don't want to pay me for my time then?"

He stared down at her, pity mixing with irritation. "I'm not looking for a date, paid or otherwise."

"Your loss." Lexi turned on her heel and started to head toward the bar where the bartender was already pouring her a rum and Coke.

He briefly wondered how many drinks it took her to get through the day. Then he silently cursed himself. Whatever her demons were, it wasn't for him to judge how she dealt with them. He followed her to the bar and took the seat next to her.

"I'm not free," she said without even looking at him.

Dax reached into his pocket and pulled out a twenty-dollar bill. "I'm looking for information."

Her eyes lit up as she focused on the cash lying between them, but as she shifted her gaze to him, they turned assessing. "It's going to cost you more than that."

The bartender chuckled as he wiped the counter. No doubt he'd witnessed her song and dance before.

"There's more where that came from if you have the information I need," Dax said.

She raised one eyebrow and took a long sip of her drink.

"I'm looking for a young shifter."

"Aren't we all, honey," she said flippantly.

"Early twenties. Highly agitated."

"Shifter with a death wish?" she asked. "Blond kid, ranting about drugs?"

"Perhaps. Have you seen him?" Dax narrowed his eyes at her, assessing if she was shoveling him a load of bullshit.

"Sure." She smiled, showing off perfectly straight, although stained, teeth. Her shoulders were relaxed, and self-confidence rolled off her in waves. If she was fucking with him, she was one really fantastic actress.

"When did you see him?"

Lexi tapped the twenty. "Gonna cost you a little more if you want answers."

If Dax hadn't been having such a shit morning, he might have laughed. He had to give her credit. She sure as hell knew how to hustle. He put a five on top of the twenty.

She frowned.

"No more until you prove you have solid information," Dax said impatiently.

She reached out to take the cash, but Dax grabbed her wrist, stopping her.

"Not until I get answers," he all but growled.

"Jesus. No need to be an asshole." Lexi jerked her hand out from under his grip. "Your boy was in here about thirty minutes ago, ranting about Allcot and the Cryrique. Seemed to think they somehow got his girlfriend killed."

Dax sucked in a sharp breath, already climbing off the stool. That was Leo all right. He was convinced someone from Cryrique was selling Scarlet on the black market. "Where did he go?"

She opened her mouth, already eyeing the money again, but before she could say anything, he added another twenty. The smile was back. "Eventually, the Cryrique building. But he said he needed answers first."

"Shit." Dax ran a hand through his thick dark hair and turned on his heel, moving toward the door. But just before he slipped out, he called over his shoulder, "What was he doing in here?"

"Lookin' for a vamp named Strix. Apparently he's the last person his girl spoke to before she overdosed." Lexi's hard exterior cracked, and she gave Dax a small, sympathetic frown. "Tell your kid I'm sorry about his girl. I've lost people I love to that poison too."

Dax gave her a short nod and strode back into the morning light. *Your kid.* Her words echoed in his mind. Is that how he saw Leo? As someone he was responsible for? Yes. He absolutely did. The younger shifter didn't have any other family, and Dax had pretty much appointed himself Leo's guardian… whether he needed one or not. And he sure as hell wasn't going to leave him hanging out to dry while he hunted down Strix, the daywalking vampire who was rumored to work for Cryrique.

Dax didn't even bother heading into Howlers. Strix wouldn't be in a shifter bar. Not unless it was filled with strippers. And Howlers wasn't that kind of place. But Dax knew exactly where to find him.

He reached for his phone and came up empty. "Fuck," he said through gritted teeth. He'd already forgotten Leo had broken the dammed thing. The hot sun beat down on the back of his neck as he took off at a dead run.

The strip club he was looking for was only five blocks away on Bourbon Street. Mornings in the French Quarter were usually eerily quiet, but not this one. Tourists were already filling the streets, out looking for breakfast and Bloody Marys to continue their vacations of debauchery. Dax ignored them all and brushed past two college kids guzzling their Huge Ass Beers to enter the strip club known as Peaches.

"Dax Marrok… Well, I didn't expect to see you in here." The woman working the front door stepped in front of him, barring him from going into the club.

He glanced down at her, taking in her pink lace push-up bra, matching hot pants, and white lace thigh-high stockings. All she needed was a bow around her neck and she'd look like a present all ready to be unwrapped. Most men would be distracted by her creamy flesh and saucy smile. He wasn't. All he saw was an obstacle. "I'm looking for someone."

"I know." She crossed her arms over her chest and didn't budge.

He narrowed his eyes and let out a small growl as he said, "Are you refusing to let me enter this establishment?"

"No." She shook her head. "Just giving you time to cool off a bit."

He itched to just pick her up and move her to the side. Instead, he leaned one shoulder against the wall and stared down at her, letting interest flash in his dark eyes as he raked his gaze down her body. "You're not exactly helping with that."

The stripper ran her fingertips over the swell of her breast and gave him a flirty smile that didn't reach her eyes.

The action told him everything he needed to know. Someone—Leo—had put her up to stalling him. He was certain of it. There was no other reason she'd know his name or try to keep him from the show on the inside. "How much did he pay you?"

"Excuse me?" She jerked her head back and feigned surprise.

"The blond shifter. Leo. How much did he pay you? I'll double it if you drop the act," Dax said, making no effort to hide his impatience.

"Fifty bucks."

It was a lie. Leo didn't have that kind of money. The kid could barely pay for his morning coffee. It didn't matter. He pulled out a wad of bills and stuffed them in her bra. "Is that enough?"

She glanced down and, without a word, stepped aside. At least he understood the language of Basin and Bourbon Street. Money was the underlying motivator. It made the area a hell of a lot easier to navigate.

Dax strode into the club. The tables were all lined with linens while the walls and chairs were all a rich peach velvet. The ornate chandeliers were set to low, giving off a soft glow as "Dancing in the Dark" played over the sound system.

Only instead of spinning around the pole, the stripper was off to the side, clutching a tiny red silk robe to her almost-naked body.

And right in the middle of the stage were Leo and Strix. The vampire had Leo in a headlock, his fangs lodged into the shifter's neck as he tried to suck the shifter dry.

Dax didn't hesitate. He flew through the air, his body already making the shift into his wolf form. His large paws hit the stage and he leaped forward, his jaws clamping down on the vampire's shoulder.

Strix immediately released Leo and let out a roar of

outrage as he turned to Dax, landing a powerful punch to his head. Dax slammed to the stage floor, but not before he took a chunk of the vampire with him.

In seconds, Dax was back on his feet, right between Strix and Leo, blood dripping from his muzzle.

"What the fuck is this?" Strix said with a hiss. "Can't a vamp enjoy his morning of tits and ass without some jackass shifter interrupting the show?"

"Fuck you and your morning!" Leo cried out, the pain radiating from him sounding like it was coming from a wounded animal. "You're a piece of shit, you know that, Strix?"

Strix just shrugged. "I never claimed to be anything other than an asshole. That's not news."

Dax clamped his jaws shut and shook his head. He was positive the vampire had no idea why Leo wanted to end his sorry existence.

"This is some fucked-up bullshit," Strix said, shaking his head to clear his shaggy black hair from his field of vision. "What happened? Did I fuck your girlfriend or something?"

A low, deadly growl came from Leo.

Strix threw his head back and laughed. "I bet that's it. What's the problem, little pup? Can't keep her satisfied now that she's been with the Strix?" He jerked one thumb at himself and came off looking like the biggest asshole to ever hit Bourbon Street.

Dax shifted back into human form, leaving himself standing between Leo and Strix, completely naked. A group of catcalls came from the dancers gathered at the wing of the stage and a couple from the back of the room. Shifters weren't modest. They spent entirely too much time shifting to worry about offending anyone with their human form.

"Word on the street is you're selling Scarlet," Dax said.

"Who said that?" he asked, making a concerted effort to stare over Dax's shoulder.

"Does it matter?" Dax asked, watching Strix carefully as he inched toward the edge of the stage.

"Sure. I should know who's spreading rumors about me." His brilliant blue eyes flashed with amusement.

A deep-seated desire to rip the vamp's head off rolled through Dax, but before he could make a move, Leo darted out from behind him, brandishing a needle.

"They aren't rumors, you piece of shit," Leo cried, waving the needle in front of Strix. "Why else would you have this on you?"

"Whoa, I—"

Leo leaped forward and grabbed the vampire by the neck, cutting off whatever it was he was going to say.

"Fuck!" Dax said just as Leo brought his arm down, clearly intending to stab Strix with his own needle.

Strix shot his hand out and grabbed Leo's wrist. The two were locked in a battle of wills, Leo trying to squeeze the life out of a vampire who couldn't die, Strix trying to crush Leo's wrist. The vampire bent Leo's arm back, causing Leo to fall to his knees and lose his grip on the vampire's neck.

"Listen, you little fucker. I don't deal. That shit is for personal use. The only girls who ever get it from me are the ones who earn it." He glanced down at his crotch. "You understand?"

Leo let out a howl and bared his teeth at the vampire.

"If you ever touch me again, I'll rip your fucking head off," Strix said through clenched teeth, only moments away from breaking Leo's arm.

Dax knew Leo had been hasty in his attack, but he

wouldn't stand by and let some lazy, drug-using, low-life vamp beat the shit out of the kid who'd just lost his girl twenty-four hours ago. There was no reasoning with either of them. Both were already too far into the fight. Instead, Dax waited for his opening, and just as he saw triumph in the vampire's expression, he lashed out. Dax's fist struck the crook of Strix's arm, breaking his connection with Leo.

Leo was knocked off-balance and fell backward as Strix spun, turning on Dax.

"You want a piece of me, pretty boy?" Strix growled.

Dax raised one eyebrow. "Did you supply Scarlet to Rhea?"

"Who the fuck is Rhea? That blond bitch who wanted to get high so bad she offered to suck me off in the alley?" he asked, disgust lining his face.

Leo let out a howl and transformed into his shifter form at the same time Dax threw another punch, connecting with the vampire's nose. There was a sickening crunch as the vampire went down. But in the very next moment, he was back on his feet, the needle Leo had dropped clutched in his fist as he rushed Dax. Leo clamped his jaws around Strix's free arm, but the vamp just kept coming.

Dax tried to dart out of the way, but the vampire was too fast, and Dax threw his arm up, trying to block the blow. A sharp stab of pain radiated through his shoulder, and a second later, he felt the burning sensation of a potent drug rushing into his bloodstream.

Euphoria took over, sending pleasure everywhere. Dax just stood there on the stage, the drug rush making his insides tingle. All the pain vanished, and Dax felt as if he were floating.

He barely heard the scramble that was going on in front

of him. He didn't care. All that mattered was the high that had propelled him into another world.

Then suddenly, Dax's blood heated and sweat coated his skin. He grew nauseated, and in the next moment his world started to turn black. *Jesus*, he thought. This is it. I'm suffering an overdose. Just like Rhea. Regret overwhelmed him. Of all the ways to go out, this had never been on his radar.

As his limbs gave out and he slumped to the floor, he thought of Phoebe and pictured the devastation on her face as she identified his cold, dead body.

Chapter Five

I climbed the stairs to the Arcane library, noting how different the structure looked in the light of day. The white columns shone in the summer sun and the windows sparkled. The place was inviting, innocuous in its almost regal architecture.

Nothing about the place said a vampire attack had happened there the night before. A chill swept over my skin as I entered the air-conditioned building. I would've brushed it off as a temperature change, but it came with an ache in the pit of my stomach and a sense of foreboding. I paused, inhaling the scent of decaying paper that always accompanied old books, and noted the dust motes swirling in the sunlight.

"Good morning, Ms. Kilsen. What can we help you with this morning?" The Arcane librarian pushed her glasses up the bridge of her nose as she smiled at me.

I glanced at her, surprised she'd remembered my name as I tried and failed to place her. I'd only been to the library a few times. The woman must've had a gifted memory. "Hello, Ms....?"

"Rolland," she supplied.

"Ms. Rolland. Thank you. I'm here to find out if you found any files associated with Simone. I was the one here after hours who found her last night. She was supposed to be helping me with some research."

Ms. Rolland frowned and shook her head. "Not that I'm aware of." She glanced at the stairs leading to the second floor. "Let's go up and see if the cleaning crew missed something."

I followed her up the wide, sweeping staircase, realizing I'd barely registered it the night before. The steps looked to be old cypress wood and had ornate railings usually only seen in the fanciest of New Orleans mansions.

"This way," the librarian said. She led the way into the same room where I'd found Simone the night before.

Sheer curtains covered the window, letting light filter in but protecting the books from the damaging sun. The carpet had been cleaned; all traces of Simone's blood was gone. The only remnant of the attack from the night before was the strong scent of industrial cleaning solvent.

"It doesn't look like any files were left here. Did you check with the cleaning crew?"

I nodded. "Yes. They gave me a report early this morning. Simone didn't have anything on her except a small handbag with her keys and her wallet."

"I see." Ms. Rolland glanced around one more time, then shook her head. "Nothing seems to be out of place, but you're welcome to take a look. While you're doing that, I'll check her search history, see if that brings anything up."

"You can do that?" I asked, surprised.

"Yep. No one gets into the database without identification."

We could do that at the Void building, but that was because no employee could log into any of the computers without their special employee code. That also meant everything we did in on the computers while in that building was traceable. I hadn't realized it was the same for the library. Good to know. I nodded an acknowledgment at her and said, "Then today might just be my lucky day."

"Take your time. I'll be downstairs at my computer, checking the database."

"Thanks." I was already turning to inspect the shelves lining the far wall.

Her heels clattered on the old wood floors as she retreated to her office, and I swept my gaze over the shelves, looking for any abnormalities. Most of the books were thick volumes, bound in leather and in pristine condition. There was nothing to indicate research that had been tucked away right before an attack. I moved methodically through the room, running my fingers lightly over the spines of the books. The Arcane was meticulous in their records, using the same smooth bindings for all of their reference books. Every single one was the same, except one. The old leather was scarred and rough under my fingertips. I paused and eyed the aged volume. The binding had no numbers, no title, and the leather had a reddish tint, lighter than the brown volumes.

Curious, I pulled the book out and quickly realized it wasn't a book at all. It was a journal. The front had the words *Secreta Secretorum* engraved in the leather.

"The Secret of Secrets," I whispered, translating the Latin phrase. I flipped it open and noted the initials on the inside of the cover: SB. There was no doubt in my mind this journal belonged to Simone Bernard. My pulse jumped as my heart quickened. Whatever information Simone had for me, likely I was holding it in my hand. I sucked in a deep breath and turned the pages.

"Son of a…" Page after page was filled with notes, all of them in Latin. I knew a few phrases, but not enough to have any idea of what the journal contained. I was going to have to translate it. After doing another sweep of the office, I tucked the journal into my messenger bag and went to find Ms. Rolland.

The librarian was sitting behind her desk, frowning as she banged away on the keys of her computer, muttering under her breath.

"Ms. Rolland?" I asked. "Is everything all right?"

She shook her head. "No. Not at all." Turning the monitor in my direction, she said, "Look at this."

The screen had a list of time-stamped log-ins, but the column where the access codes would normally go was completely blank. "Whoa. That's not right."

She gritted her teeth and punched another key. Her name and access number flashed up on the screen. "This is yesterday. Notice anything unusual?"

Her log-in history was missing. I met her eyes, registering the anger mixed with frustration staring back at me. "Looks like all your records have been wiped."

"Completely. The entire month is gone, and it was there yesterday. I know. I checked when I was updating records. It looks like whoever attacked Simone is covering something up. Bastard. I can't believe he breached our security, and from the looks of this, he's going to get away with it."

"Not so fast." I pulled the journal out of my bag and slid it across her desk. "I found this upstairs." After opening the front cover, I tapped on Simone's initials. "I don't read Latin, but I'm pretty sure that after I translate her notes, I'll be able to connect some dots. If Allcot and his band of vampires are trying to keep whatever information Simone has secret, it will be fairly obvious once we uncover the material."

The frustration drained from the librarian's face and her body visibly relaxed as she sat back in her chair. "How did you manage to find this? I swear, I checked three times to make sure Simone didn't leave anything behind."

I gave her a cat-that-ate-the-canary grin. "Simone hid it on one of the bookshelves. I imagine she chose the library as a meeting place precisely because it would be easy to hide this should anything go wrong. And lucky for her, I'm very good at my job."

"There's no question there." She scanned the pages again, this time concentrating on the text. After a minute of trying to read the scribble inside, she shook her head. "Nope. Can't recall enough to make this out. But I can translate it for you. I'd just need a little time to get through it."

"I've got it," I said, unwilling to let the text out of my sight. The journal was the closest thing I had to possibly finding out what might have happened to my brother. There was no way I was giving it up. I nodded to her computer. "I'll let IT know you need someone to analyze the data breach. It could just be a glitch."

She pursed her lips into a thin line, and I knew she was thinking the same thing I was: the wipe had been deliberate. But until we had cold hard facts, there wasn't anything we could do about it. Hopefully IT would be able to trace when and where the wipe had occurred. It would help us track down the hacker.

"Don't worry. The Void guys will get to the bottom of this." I tried to reassure her.

"They'd better," Ms. Rolland said, her expression grave. "Otherwise, the information in this library is about to become a huge liability."

I glanced around, wondering just how hard it would be to hack into sensitive Void records. Then I shook my head. There was no point worrying about what could happen until we knew what we were working with. I pulled my phone out, ready to call the office when the device started ringing and the director's number flashed on the screen.

"Halston?" I asked when I answered.

"It's Maria," Halston's assistant said. "There's been an emergency. You need to get back to the Void right away."

"What's wrong?" I asked, then whispered to Ms. Rolland, "I have to go. It's urgent."

She gestured for me to take my leave, and I was already striding out of the building when Maria said, "It's your partner, Marrok. He's been attacked and is suffering an overdose of Scarlet."

"What?" I cried into the phone even as I took off at a dead run. "Scarlet? That's impossible. Dax hates drugs."

"He didn't take it voluntarily. At least not according to Leo, the shifter who brought him in. It happened during a fight with a vampire."

Pure rage surged through my veins, heating me from the inside out. I sped up, lengthening my strides, and said, "I'll be there in five minutes."

Chapter Six

I ran through the Void building, my boots echoing on the tile floors. It was hard to breathe, not because I was out of shape or pushing too hard. No. My heart was lodged in my throat as I pictured Dax lying unconscious in the medical unit. A Scarlet overdose? How the fuck had that happened?

As I rounded the corner, Leo's distressed howl reverberated from Dax's room, and I prayed to the goddess that Dax was still alive. As long as he was alive, there was hope. My stomach roiled, and bile rose in the back of my throat. I never had been very good at hope.

"Dax?" I cried as I burst through the door and rushed to his side. An IV had been administered, and machines were monitoring his heart rate and blood pressure. The steady *beep, beep, beep* went a long way in calming my fears. He was alive. Thank the gods.

But he was so pale, his skin ashen, and his eyes sunken as if he was on the verge of death. "Jesus, Dax. What happened to you?" I asked, taking his cold hand in mine.

Leo let out a low growl and fisted his hands in his hair as he prowled around the room. "It's my fault. It's always my fault."

"What do you mean?" I asked him, keeping my eye trained on Dax. "What happened, Leo?"

"You're going to hate me."

"Only if you don't tell me exactly what happened," I snapped, turning to glare at him. Now was not the time for self-pity. "I can't help him if I don't know the details."

Leo paused on the other side of Dax's hospital bed and dropped his hands from his head. He stood perfectly still, staring at me as he said, "I tracked down the vamp who sold Rhea the drugs. I wanted answers—"

"You wanted revenge." I corrected him, my tone void of judgment.

His tortured eyes met mine and he nodded. "Yeah. Revenge. I wanted him to suffer."

"Did he?" I asked, wishing with all my heart that he had.

Leo shook his head. "No. Not really. He was old and fast, and soon after I attacked him, I knew I was in over my head."

I swept my gaze over the younger shifter, relieved to see he was mostly intact. The only evidence of the vamp attack were the bites and bruises on his neck. "But then Dax showed up, and the vamp went after him instead," I guessed.

"Not exactly. But you're close. I tried to stab the vampire with his own needle, but he got the better of me and was moments from beating the shit out of me when Dax stepped in. I must've dropped the needle because the next thing I knew, Strix had it in his hand and attacked Dax with it."

"Strix?" I asked, the name sounding familiar. "Is he one of Allcot's?"

"That's the word on the street, but he's always either on

Basin Street pushing that shit of his or in the strip clubs on Bourbon all day. Though he claims he isn't dealing. Fucking liar. I'd bet my last dollar he sells to anyone who comes knocking."

"Dark hair, looks like he belongs in an eighties hair band?" I asked.

Leo shrugged. "More like a street punk who hasn't showered in days."

I nodded. That sounded about right. Though if he was that visible, it was hard to believe he was still one of Allcot's. The powerful vampire wasn't above employing dealers, he just usually demanded they were discreet. I filed that information away for later and turned my attention back to Dax.

"What did the healer say? Is he going to wake up?" Just asking the question made me feel hollow. Dax was my partner and on again, off again lover. We'd just recently turned the switch to on again. And, I guess, technically we were dating. But it was so much more than that. Dax was my partner. The person I relied on day in and day out to have my back. There was a level of trust there I'd never had with anyone else of the opposite sex. Was it love? I didn't know. Maybe. But losing him wasn't an option.

Leo stared down at Dax, clutching the metal railing at the foot of the bed. "They don't— Argh!" Leo's eyes turned yellow as he prowled around the room, a sure sign he was losing control to his inner wolf.

"Leo—" I started, alarmed that he was able to shift at all. Hadn't security forced him to go through the magical neutralizer when he'd entered the building? His ability to shift should've been out of commission for at least a couple of hours.

He crashed into the wall and let out a roar as his body contorted and his bones cracked and reformed into his shifter shape. His wolf had taken over, and it was clear from how he was twisting and fighting the transformation that he wasn't in control of the shift.

That wasn't good. Too much had happened over the past couple of days. His girl had died and now the person who'd taken on the role as a pseudo father was in a drug-induced coma. Leo had no one save Dax and by extension me. The stress of losing those close to him had gotten the better of him.

I darted out of the room and ran smack into Talisen, a fae and healer who also happened to be my best friend's husband. He'd recently started working for the Void again as a researcher in their medical labs. He was particularly gifted with stone and crystal magic and had proven to be a valuable asset because of his ability to discern new healing techniques.

"Phoebe, are you all right?" he asked, gripping both my arms as he scanned his gaze down my body.

"I'm fine," I said, shaking him off. "It's Leo. He got so agitated he spontaneously shifted and now he's completely out of control. Didn't they make him go through security?"

A loud crash came from Dax's room, followed by another howl.

"Damn. I was afraid of that. His wolf must've already been highly agitated when he went through the machine. And since wolves are the most resistant to the neutralizer of us paranormals, his wolf likely fought off the magic and he wasn't affected at all." Talisen grabbed a light-rose-colored stone from a pocket of his lab coat and strode into the room.

I followed and stood in the doorway, magic pulsing at my fingertips, ready to help should Talisen need backup. The room was in shambles. The heart monitor had been knocked over, the IV line had been ripped out of Dax's arm, and all the supplies that had been neatly stacked on the counter had been overturned and were now strewn across the floor. Dax and his bed appeared to be the only two things that had survived Leo's wrath.

Talisen calmly moved toward Leo, forcing the wolf back into a corner. Leo's hackles rose and he bared his teeth at Talisen, but the fae was unfazed. He just pointed his rose stone at the wolf and said, "*Somnum.*"

The wolf blinked, then suddenly he slid to the floor, his paws stretched out in front of him and his head resting on the tile with his eyes closed.

"Sleeping spell?" I asked.

"Yes." He walked over and crouched down next to the wolf. After searching for a pulse, he nodded and said, "He's going to need to sleep this one off."

"I'm on it." I called security. When they answered, I said, "We have a wolf that needs to spend some time in a containment cell."

A moment later, I ended the call and looked up into Tal's concerned expression.

"Do you think that's necessary?" he asked.

"Absolutely. Have you ever seen a wolf come out of a spell-induced sleep? Not just heard about it, but seen it with your own two eyes?"

"No, I guess I haven't," he admitted. "Though I've certainly been around ones who've passed out from too many drugs, too many drinks, too much everything. It's been fine."

"They sometimes wake up in a disoriented rage too. He needs a room where he can be monitored and administered sedatives if the break persists."

Talisen frowned, clearly unhappy with my explanation, but he nodded and waited with me until two guards arrived and hauled the limp shifter away. "How much do you trust them?" he asked me as we watched the two guards disappear around the corner.

I chewed on my lower lip. "It's not the guards we need to be wary of. It's the system itself. If they think he's a danger to anyone, they'll pump him full of drugs and keep him that way until someone intervenes."

"Damn," he said, running a hand through his short blond hair.

"We'll keep an eye on him. For now, tell me about Dax. How is he?"

Talisen tugged me back into Dax's room and immediately righted the equipment and got my partner hooked back up to the IV and heart monitor. That reassuring *beep, beep, beep* filled the room again, and it was as if I could feel my blood pressure returning to normal.

"I have good news and bad news," Talisen said, taking a seat on one of the rolling stools as he manually checked Dax's vitals.

I closed my eyes and took a deep breath. "Okay, lay it on me."

"The good news is that Dax has mostly already metabolized the drug out of his system, and he appears to be stable."

My partner didn't look any better than he had when I'd walked into the room twenty minutes ago. "Okay. So it's obviously had an effect on him. How long until he recovers?"

A muscle in Talisen's jaw pulsed. Definitely not a good sign. It was one of his tells when something was bothering him.

"Tal? I need to know."

He ground his teeth and forced out, "That's the problem. I don't have an answer. I did a tox screen, and while there are traces of the drug still in his bloodstream, it isn't enough to warrant this." He waved a hand at Dax. "So I had the techs run a few more tests, and they found something that presents as a poison."

"Poison?" I gasped out. "You think the drug was laced with something toxic?"

He nodded. "It's the only explanation for his reaction to it. We have to run some more tests to see if we can pinpoint it. But Phoebe, I have to warn you that the symptoms he's exhibiting right now indicate that if this doesn't clear within the next twenty-four hours, whatever is causing this could be fatal."

"Twenty-four hours?" I choked out. My mouth had gone dry while a chill ran down my spine. I stared at Dax and felt the foreboding kick in again.

"We'll know more once I'm done in the lab." He squeezed my hand, then quietly slipped out of the room.

I sat on the edge of Dax's bed, trying to get my shit together. Leo had been hauled off to a cage somewhere while Tal was playing scientist in the lab. And here I was on the verge of my own fucking breakdown. First my brother had suddenly appeared after eight long years. Then he disappeared right before my eyes. Now Dax's life was in danger. And all I felt was helpless.

Of all the skills I possessed, bringing my shifter boyfriend back from the brink of death, wasn't one of them. That was Talisen's domain... and maybe Healer Imogen's. She was a gifted healer with a new practice in New Orleans. She also did work for Cryrique. I pulled out my phone and scrolled through my contacts, hovering over her name. Should I call her? She didn't work for the Void. The director would be pissed if I brought in someone from the outside. Especially someone with ties to Allcot.

I glanced at Dax again, taking in his lifeless form. I knew then that I'd call the other healer if my back was against the wall, but I owed it to the director to at least ask her first. Leaning down, I brushed my lips over his forehead and said, "You better wake up. I'm not standing for this weak-ass bullshit where you lie around in a hospital bed while I tackle this next case by myself. You hear me?"

There was no response from my shifter. Not even an elevated heart rate. Sighing, I brushed his hair out of his eyes, then turned and headed for the director's office.

"KILSEN. GOOD, YOU'RE HERE," Director Halston said as I strode into her office. She made a note in a file and waved at one of the chairs in front of her desk.

I shook my head. "I'll stand."

"Suit yourself," she said, her voice clipped. "There's been a development in the case I gave you this morning."

"You're kidding." My eyebrows shot up. "I haven't even started working on it yet."

"I know. I was just alerted to a case up in Jackson that might mirror our investigation. There's been a shifter who was given what they thought was a fatal dose of Scarlet. Only he didn't die. He was in a coma, and when he woke up, he appeared to be fine. Seven days later, he went insane and killed half his pack."

Her words hit me with such force I felt like I'd been

sucker punched in the gut, and I slowly lowered myself to the metal chair behind me. It was a weak reaction. I was a powerful witch. A vampire hunter. I'd recently stopped a war between vampires and shifters. Frankly, I was a badass. But the thought of losing Dax had all but paralyzed me. "Killed them how?"

She looked up from her file and stared me straight in the eye. "He just snapped. One minute he was enjoying a barbeque with his buddies and the next he was ripping throats out. No one survived."

"Not even the shifter?" I asked, fighting the urge to press my hand to my throat in horror. I'd already shown enough weakness in this meeting. If the director thought I was falling apart, she'd replace me in two seconds flat. And that was unacceptable. I was going to hunt down Strix and whoever was responsible for Rhea's death and make them pay. It would be very inconvenient if I was taken out of the field and assigned to a desk.

She pressed her lips into a thin line as she shook her head. "The Void branch had to put him down."

"Christ," I said, blinking in disbelief. "How could they…" I let out a long breath and added, "Never mind. They did what they had to do."

"Just as you would, Kilsen," she said with a nod.

It was good to know the director had confidence in me. Because I sure the hell didn't. If I was the one holding the sword and Dax was the one I had to slay, I honestly didn't know if I could strike the final blow. Sure, I could kick his ass from here to Sunday, but kill him? No. I didn't think so.

The director and I stared at each other, and I had a moment to wonder what she was thinking. Her expression was hard and determined, just the way it was every day. The director didn't let shit get to her. Or if she did, she never let it show. It was a trait I admired and one I tried hard to mimic. I usually did too, right up until my small circle of friends ended up in the middle of the fray.

"There's more," she said.

I blinked, forcing myself to focus. "I'm listening."

"Those five other shifters who survived their overdoses, you need to bring them in. We need to monitor them until we're sure they won't succumb to the same fate."

I sucked in a sharp breath. "And Dax? Will you force him to stay here too?" Assuming he woke up from his coma. But I wasn't willing to voice my fear. I didn't even want to consider such a horrible outcome.

She drummed her fingers on her desk, contemplating my question. "Under normal circumstances we would, but he has contacts with the shifter community. And we need all hands on deck. When he wakes, and if he's able, he can work with you. But you should be prepared if he loses control," Halston said. "Can you do that?"

"Yes." There was no hesitation. As much as I cared for him, if he lost it and started hurting people, I'd stop him. I'd find a way to incapacitate him until the healers found a solution to his madness. One way or another, I'd do what I had to in order to protect the people of New Orleans.

She stood and leaned over her desk as she pierced me with her stare. "I'm counting on you to make sure you find an antidote and/or keep your partner in line once he wakes up. There will not be innocent blood on our hands. Understood?"

She didn't need to tell me twice. I got to my feet, determination filling all my hollow spaces. "Got it. In order to make sure we've exhausted every lead that may help us keep

Dax's inner wolf in check, I'd like to bring Healer Imogen in to take a look at him."

She raised a skeptical eyebrow. "Allcot's witch?"

I nodded, not even bothering to argue her status. I wasn't exactly sure what Imogen was doing for the powerful vampire, but as we both well knew, no association with Allcot came without strings. If she wasn't already doing him favors, she soon would be. Just like how I'd turned a blind eye to some of his dealings in New Orleans because he'd been protecting Willow's pseudo sister-in-law and her nephew from those who would use Beau Junior's gifts to their advantage. I wasn't ashamed of what I did or didn't do for the vampire. I did what I had to, just like everyone else in this corrupt town.

"What about Talisen Kavanagh? You don't think he's got the chops to deal with this?" she asked.

"It's not that I don't think Tal can handle it, it's just that I think Imogen likely has more knowledge in this particular case. The sooner we know the specifics, the sooner we can get Dax back on his feet. And she can probably help with the other five shifters who suffered an overdose once we track them down. Maybe let her check them over and see if there are any similarities in their condition or warning signs they're about to lose control."

The director sucked in a deep breath through her nose. A bad sign. That meant she was gearing up to give 101 reasons why the answer was no.

"Allcot owes me a favor," I said, referring to the fact that I'd recently helped him save his consort from an insane shifter and a youth-obsessed sorceress. "If I show up with her at my side to collect the favor, it's much more likely he'll share any information he might have about the drug with her. The more information we have, the better Dax's chances will be to survive this. Allcot won't trust Talisen with the same information."

The director slowly sat back in her chair. After a moment, she nodded, though there was no denying the reluctance in her gray eyes. "Fine. I'll let you consult with her on Marrok's case, but she signs a nondisclosure, and I want you to keep her on a need-to-know basis. No details about the vamp who attacked Marrok, and definitely don't let on that we're investigating the trafficking of this drug. If Allcot is behind it, we don't want him alerted."

"Got it." I stood and strode toward the door, already itching to get back to Dax's side.

"Kilsen?"

I paused and glanced back. "Yes?"

"If you're too emotionally invested, tell me now. I'll get another agent on this. I— The Void can't afford the PR nightmare that would come with a mass murdering of the city's shifters."

I stood completely still, processing what she'd just said. PR nightmare? That was what she was worried about? Disgust and hatred for the system, the politics, and the cold, calculating nature of the director rose up and nearly made me lash out. How dare she reduce Dax's critical condition down to what it would look like should too many shifters die? But I knew that if I let my true feelings show, I'd be benched so fast my ass would be full of splinters. I gave her a tight smile, one I knew must've looked more like grim acceptance than anything else. "I'm fine. I've got this."

She leaned back in her chair, seemingly relieved by my response, and picked up the phone. Without another word to me, she hit a button and said, "Get Senator Quinton on the line."

Chapter Seven

$\mathscr{I}$ leaned against the nondescript brick building in the heart of the Irish Channel and watched the gorgeous woman with the porcelain skin gracefully exit her white BMW. Allcot was definitely taking care of his bought-and-paid-for healer. She was dressed in an expensive-looking tailored suit and wore black Louis Vuitton high heels.

Healer Imogen grabbed her leather satchel out of the back seat, then turned and gave me a big smile as she waved, clearly pleased to see me. I waved back but couldn't match her enthusiasm. I'd just come from Dax's room, and his skin was taking on a grayish tone. If I hadn't felt his pulse, I'd have been certain we'd already lost him. Talisen was doing everything he could to keep Dax breathing, but it was obvious he was in over his head.

"I hope you have some serious tricks up your sleeve, because Dax is going to need them," I said, handing her the nondisclosure agreement. "You need to sign this before I can let you in the building."

She glanced down at it and frowned. "The director doesn't trust me."

It wasn't a question, just a statement. "The director doesn't trust anybody. That can't be a surprise. I'm sure Allcot had you sign something similar."

She shrugged one shoulder, making a noncommittal gesture, then read the simple one-page NDA. It basically said anything she saw or heard while doing work for or with the Void was confidential. She pulled out a pen, scribbled her name at the bottom, and handed it back to me.

"Thanks." I clutched the paperwork in one hand as I led the way through the glass doors toward the security screening area. "She's going through with me," I told the guard as I gestured for her to hand over her satchel.

"You know we can't allow that," he said, stepping in front of me and crossing his arms. "She needs to go through the neutralizer like everyone else."

I narrowed my eyes. "She's a goddamned healer, Frank. If you neutralize her, you'll be fucking up the entire reason I brought her here."

The neutralizer was the screening that zapped a supernatural being's power, rendering them mostly harmless while they were in the Void building. It wasn't pleasant and left a person feeling like their life force had all but been ripped from them.

"She's here for Marrok," Frank's partner pointed out.

Frank just shrugged. "I don't give a fuck about some egotistical piece-of-trash shifter who thinks he's better than me just because he was born with an eight-pack and has women falling at his feet."

I stared at the portly security guard and would've laughed

if I wasn't so pissed off. "Your insecurity is showing, Frank. Now step aside. Imogen and I have work to do."

He still didn't budge. His partner *tsked* and shook his head as he retreated, clearly knowing what was coming next.

"I'm not letting her through unless the director herself comes down and approves this. Even then I might put that bag of hers through the neutralizer," Frank said. "I don't care if she does have perky breasts and an ass most men would sell their soul for. No one is getting the jump on me."

"I am," I said, too pissed off to care that I'd likely be sanctioned for my actions. Without any warning, I reached out and grabbed him by the neck. And even though he weighed well over two hundred pounds, my magic kicked in and with hardly any effort at all, I threw him against the wall and watched him crumple to the floor. "That's for holding us up and judging Imogen on her tits and ass. Next time, keep your bullshit observations to yourself, jackass."

"This is how your coworkers treat you?" Imogen asked with an air of disbelief as she followed me through the nonmagical metal detector. "No wonder you're cranky so often."

I glanced back at her and let out a surprised bark of laughter. "Usually they're cool. It's just that Frank there was dumped by his shifter girlfriend a few weeks ago, and now he apparently has a grudge against the entire species."

"Shifters are trash," Frank called from where he was still slumped against the wall. "She left me over ten pounds. Ten fucking pounds. Shallow bitch," he muttered.

I glanced at Bernard. "Get him an appointment with the Void's psychologist, will you? If he behaves like that to someone less understanding, he's really going to get his ass kicked."

"I'm already on it. Yesterday he cussed out the director's assistant. It wasn't pretty," Bernard said.

"Christ." I shook my head. "Poor Maria. Did she tell the director?"

"No. I don't think so. But she did threaten to spell his dick off if he spoke to her that way again. I don't think she was kidding either."

I snorted. "Serves him right." I waved a goodbye and ushered Imogen to the elevator.

"Really get his ass kicked?" Imogen asked, taking strides so long she was quickly going to outpace me. "What do you call that back there?"

I quickened my steps. "I was just putting him in his place. He's a power-hungry douche canoe. I'll be damned if I'm going to take his shit."

"You didn't want to report him?" she asked curiously, following me into the elevator.

I took a moment to consider her question as the elevator shot up three floors. "I probably should in order to start the paper trail, but I'm guessing he won't fuck with me again. Not after that. He won't want me to embarrass him, which I will because I'm about a hundred times more powerful than he is."

"Is he a witch?" she asked, frowning. "I didn't feel any magical energy streaming from him."

It was a valid question. Just as I'd felt Simone's power and Dax's neighbor's power, Frank's should've been giving off something. I'd never felt anything from him. "I'm told he has some witch blood, but as far as I know, his only power is being able to sense the abilities of other supernaturals. It's likely why he was insisting you go through the neutralizer. You have too much power and it makes him uncomfortable."

"Interesting." She clutched her healer's bag. "It's hard to imagine someone so surly keeping his job."

I shrugged. "He used to be good at it. Now he's a jackass." I opened Dax's door and said, "Forget Frank. Dax is in here."

Imogen slipped into the room and immediately moved to Dax's side. She took one look at him, then glanced up at me. "This isn't good. I'm going to need your help. Now."

I hurried over to the other side of the bed so that I was standing across from her and waited for instructions. Imogen had used my magic to boost her healing energy before. There was no reason to believe it couldn't work again. I glanced down at Dax's ghostly face and cursed myself for letting Frank waste precious moments down in the lobby. If anything happened to Dax, that dickhead was going to pay big-time.

"I need your hands here," Imogen said, nodding to her hands that she'd already placed over Dax's heart.

I slipped my chilled fingers over her warm ones and waited.

Her piercing blue eyes stared right through me as she appeared lost in concentration. Magic sparked at her fingertips, instantly drawing power from mine. "That's it," she whispered, her tone ethereal. "Just let the magic flow freely."

My instinct was to call up every last drop of power I possessed. If she needed it to heal Dax, then she could have it, do whatever she wanted to with it. I didn't care just as long as she brought him out of the drug-induced coma. But I didn't want to unleash more than she was ready for, so I tried to relax and just let my magic naturally fuse with hers.

"Yes, just like that," she said as her body gently swayed back and forth. "Perfect, Phoebe."

Her words only added to my frustration. I didn't want to be gentle or engage in some sort of new age magic ritual. I wanted to kick someone's ass. Beat down the vampire who was responsible for this nightmare.

The collective magic intensified, and despite the fact we were in a windowless room, a wind picked up, blowing Imogen's long auburn hair out behind her. "Now, Phoebe," she ordered. "Send in every bit of light you possess. He needs it now."

"Light?" I asked.

"Yes, we need to pull him from the darkness. Now, Phoebe. Do it now!" Thunder rumbled through the room as her hair started to rise from the static electricity. I focused on the agate set in the bracelet at my wrist, then imagined using it to blast the vampire who'd done this to Dax.

A brilliant bright light flashed beneath our joined hands then hovered for a moment over his skin like an oil slick.

"No, dammit!" I cried, still trying to pour my magic into Imogen's fingers. I caught her worried expression and felt my heart nearly break in two. "This is not how he's going to go out. Do you understand me?"

"Of course he isn't," she said calmly. "Your love is going to keep him here."

I rolled my eyes. "Don't start with that bullshit. Love isn't the magical answer to everything. Besides, we're not in love. We're just screwing."

"Are you sure about that?" she asked with a self-satisfied smile just as Dax sucked in a deep breath and his eyes fluttered open. She glanced down at him, her smile turning to a grin. "Welcome back, Daxon. I don't mind telling you we were really worried about you there for a moment."

"Dax!" I cried out and grabbed his hand, my magical light still flashing from my fingertips.

"Ouch," he croaked out, his voice cracking as he turned his face to shield his eyes from the bright light.

"Oh no. I'm sorry." I yanked my hands back and turned my focus inward to calm my magic.

"It's Phoebe who brought you back, Dax," Imogen said, leaning down to check his pupils with a tiny penlight.

"Dammit," he said through a growl. "Can I have a minute?"

"Nope," she said cheerfully. "Need to log your vitals so I can get a baseline and see where we're at."

I reached out and took one of his hands in both of mine again and sat on a stool, grinning at him like a fool. After Imogen moved on to checking his blood pressure, I said, "Hey there."

He turned his head, and his dark eyes focused on me. He was quiet while he studied my face. "You're smiling, but something's wrong. What happened? Why am I here?"

I'd been expecting his memory to be faulty. He had been in a coma after all. "You broke up an altercation between Leo and Strix. The vampire got the jump on you and stabbed you with a syringe full of Scarlet."

"Fuck," he said, running the back of his hand over his forehead.

"Exactly. You went into a coma and you were only getting worse as the day wore on. Imogen here was the one who saved your ass."

"She's being modest," Imogen said with a kind smile. "Without her light, there'd have been no path out of the darkness."

I stared at her, wondering when she'd turned into some

sort of new age philosopher. She caught my eye and shrugged as if to say she didn't know either.

Dax cleared his throat. "Where's Leo?"

I grimaced.

"Phoebe?" he pressed. "Is he all right?"

"Sure. I mean, he's safe."

"Safe?" Dax wasn't buying any of my stall tactics.

"Listen, his wolf got the better of him, and we had to put him in a cell for his own safety."

He closed his eyes and shook his head as he whispered, "Dammit." Then his eyes flew open and he focused on me. "Are you sure he's all right? When's the last time you saw him?"

The sounds from the heart monitor started to speed up, and that steady *beep, beep, beep* that had been so comforting was really starting to annoy me. "Not since they took him out of here. I—"

"What the fuck, Phoebe?" he said, pushing himself up into a sitting position. His color had returned to normal, and any weakness he'd suffered from the drug appeared to have vanished. "Why the hell haven't you checked on him? You know they stuff wolves in cages and just leave them there until someone takes responsibility for them. Hasn't the kid had enough trauma over the past few days? We can't just—"

"Enough!" I held a hand up and shook my head at him. "Do you really want to know why I'm not sitting downstairs babysitting your stray wolf?"

"Dammit, Phoebe. You don't need to put it like that. Babysitting? Really?" A scowl spread across his face and there was no denying he was seriously annoyed. "You know they lock us shifters in cold, dank cages, right?"

Of course I knew. I'd worked at the Void long before Dax

had come along. I was intimately familiar with just how awful those cages could be. Willow and her pup Link had been locked up in the basement a few years ago for days after the director had been spelled to carry out someone else's sinister agenda. Interestingly enough, it had been Allcot and his son who'd helped me free Willow and Link. I was well versed on just how bad things could get. Annoyed that he'd started in on me about Leo almost immediately, I turned to him and said, "Dax… shut up."

His mouth worked as he tried to come up with a reply to my childish outburst.

But before he could say anything, I added, "You almost died. In fact, if Imogen hadn't gotten here when she did, the worst would've probably happened. I've spent the past two hours trying to narrow down the effects of the drug on you, convincing the director to let Imogen try to help, and worrying my ass off right here at your bedside. So don't guilt me about not keeping an eye on Leo. He's here, in the Void, and not posing a danger to anyone. Now that you appear to be back among the living, I'll go see him and find out if they were able to stabilize him enough for him to shift back into human form. If so, I'll bring him in to see you."

Dax blinked, glanced between me and Imogen, then shook his head. "Sorry. Clearly I had no idea how bad it was."

Imogen handed him what looked like a vitamin pack. "Take this. It will help get your strength up."

The door swung open and Talisen rushed in. As soon as he saw us, he paused and then let out a sigh of relief. "Thank the gods."

"What is it?" I asked, confused.

He held up a monitor, showing some sort of reading with

a giant spike. "I thought Dax had a heart attack and I got up here as soon as I could."

"These two did something," Dax said, waving a hand at me and Imogen. "Not sure what, but I seem to be okay."

"For now," I said with a heavy heart, then explained to them what the director had told me about the possibility of the toxin turning him insane. When I finished, there was a hush of silence.

Finally, Dax swung his legs over the side of the bed and stood. "Well, if I only have seven days, I have some things to take care of."

"Dax—"

"Don't worry, Phoebs," he said with a wink. "I'll leave the Trooper in your care."

"Goddammit." I shook my head. "Stop talking like that. We're going to figure this out."

"Right," Talisen added, turning to Imogen. "Do you know anything about this drug? Because I've been running some tests and I have a few theories. Maybe I can run them by you?"

"A little bit," she said. "I've had some clients who were addicted to it, and I have access to medical journals and other resources."

Other resources. She was talking about Cryrique. It was the main reason I'd wanted to bring her in on this investigation.

"Okay then." Tal held his arm out to her. "Let's get to the lab and see what we can do."

Imogen turned to me with one eyebrow raised.

"Go ahead," I said. "The more we know about the drug, the better. Come up with some sort of antidote while you're down there too, okay?"

"We're on it," Talisen said as he led the other healer out of the room.

Once they were gone, Dax glanced at me, all traces of humor gone. "How bad is this really?"

I sat down on the bed next to him, our thighs barely touching, and said, "It's bad, Dax. Of the nine shifters we know who've OD'd on this shit, three have perished and another was terminated after he went insane. The director has tasked us with finding the other five and bringing them in just in case they suffer the same fate."

"And what about me? What if I'm infected?" he asked, twining his fingers with mine.

I stared down at our connection, squeezed his hand, and said, "The director has made me responsible for you and your actions until we figure this out. So keep your shit together, all right?"

He turned and stared me in the eye. "Does that mean what I think it means?"

"That I'll be staying at your house from now on? Yep. Get used to it. I require clean sheets and toilets."

He snorted out a huff of laughter. "You got it."

That silence fell between us again, neither of us wanting to voice the reality of what would happen if he lost control of his inner wolf. It didn't matter that I'd been ordered to take him out if the worst happened. It's what he'd expect of me anyway.

"You scared me there for a minute," I said softly.

"Just a minute?" he asked, caressing the back of my hand with this thumb.

"Maybe two." I gave him a wry smile, then sobered. "Seriously, don't do that again. I don't think my heart can take it."

He tilted his head down and gave me a kiss on the top of my head. "I won't. I'm not going anywhere."

I reached up and pressed my hand to his cheek. "Good, because I've gotten used to having you around."

A glint flashed in his dark eyes as he gazed down at me, his expression tender and full of emotion. My heart swelled, and I wondered if the warmth coursing through my body was what everyone called love. I pressed my lips to his and buried my other hand in his thick hair, needing that physical connection. His arms came around me, and suddenly I just felt safe and at home, right where I was supposed to be.

The kiss was slow and tender, and I knew then I was a goner.

I pulled away and cleared my throat as I slid off the bed. The wall clock ticked, catching my attention. The day had slipped by, and it was well into the afternoon. "Get back in that bed and get some more rest. I'm going to go check on Leo, make sure he's okay and let him know you're awake."

Dax shook his head and got to his feet. "I'm going with you."

"But—" I started.

"Phoebe," he said, pressing my hand to his chest over his steady heartbeat. "I'm fine… at least for now. Let's go. We need to see Leo, and then we have a case to solve."

He was so steady, so confident and sure of himself. How could I argue with that?

"Okay then. Put some pants on and we'll get moving."

He glanced down at his short medical gown and chuckled as he ripped it off, revealing his perfectly sculpted naked body. It was no wonder Frank was so bitter. What mortal could compete with the likes of that?

"You're staring." Dax pulled on a fresh pair of jeans from the well-stocked closet.

"Yep," I said, unashamed.

"Like what you see?" he asked, grinning over his shoulder as he grabbed a T-shirt.

"You already know the answer to that." I walked up behind him, cupped my hand over his ass, and whispered, "Later tonight, I'll show you just how much."

Chapter Eight

The steep stone steps led to a dreary, cold basement. One fluorescent light swung from the middle of the room while steel cages lined the wall on the right. Rage, tied to injustice and discrimination, welled in Dax's chest. It took everything he had to swallow the frustration that always tried to choke him when he had to deal with caged wolves.

While Dax worked for the Arcane, the organization had a long history of discrimination against shifters. A century ago, shifters had still been seen as animals, second-class citizens who were inferior to all other supernatural beings. In those days, more often than not when shifters were arrested, the charges were bogus. Then they were thrown in cages just like the ones lining the walls of the Void's basement, and they were left there until they either went crazy or confessed to a crime they hadn't committed just to be moved to better conditions.

"There he is." Phoebe pointed to the shadow in the corner of the closest cage.

Seeing Leo locked up made his blood boil. The young

shifter was curled up on the stone floor, naked, no blanket, no clothes in sight. He'd clearly been thrown in the cage and left without regard to anything other than locking him up.

Leo lifted his head and blinked a couple of times.

"You okay, man?" Dax asked him, crouching down to see him at eye level.

"Dax?" Leo blinked then jumped to his feet to hurry over to the bars. "You're okay?"

"I seem to be," he said, rising back up to standing position. "What about you? I heard your inner wolf got a little wild today."

Leo hung his head in shame as he nodded. "I didn't mean to let it happen, I just… It was a bad day."

"You can say that again," Phoebe said, giving him a sympathetic smile. "How long have you been back?"

He shrugged. "No idea. Too dark to tell time. No one has been down here except you two. A couple of hours maybe? Am I getting out of here?"

Dax shared a glance with Phoebe. No one had cleared Leo to leave, and if history was a predictor of the future, the Void wasn't going to be too hot on the idea. Not after he'd already lost his shit.

"That's a no, right?" Leo started to pace. His limbs became jerky and he grumbled under his breath about never getting a fair shake.

"Leo, listen," Phoebe said. "No one has said anything either way. As far as I know, they just put you here to keep everyone, including you, safe while you slept off the sleeping spell. We need to get a psych consult down here to see where we go from here."

The young shifter snorted his derision. "Psych consult. Right." He stomped around, fisting one hand in his hair much like he'd done earlier in Dax's room. "I guess I should just get real comfy here, because no one is gonna let a fuckup like me back out on the streets."

"I think if you—" Phoebe started.

"Who cares what you think?" Leo roared, his eyes watering and his body so tense he was vibrating. "I am nothing. Worthless. Don't you understand that? They don't care about me. I'm just a shifter with no roots, no money, no education. You think they're gonna—"

"That's enough," Dax said, his voice low but full of authority.

Leo clamped his mouth shut and stared down at the ground.

Good, Dax thought. That meant the pup actually saw him as an alpha. That would bode well for him when arguing to get him out. "They will never let you leave if you're just going to rant like a maniac. Like it or not, you are dangerous. We all are. And it doesn't matter what your intent is. If you can't control yourself, the Void has every right to think the city is better off with you off the streets. Unless you can contain that inner wolf of yours, you'll likely find yourself institutionalized. Do you want that?"

"They can't do that to me," Leo said. But his voice wavered, and it was clear he wasn't at all confident in his statement.

"They can, and they will," Phoebe said. "The Void's mission is to police the supernatural activity in New Orleans. They have broad power. And while I don't agree with these conditions"—she waved a hand indicating the dank basement —"I do understand that they'll do what they have to."

"It's up to you to change their minds," Dax told Leo.

The shifter rolled his shoulders and stretched his neck,

visibly trying to ease the tension in his frame. Then he met Dax's gaze and said, "I don't want to be locked up."

Dax nodded, grabbed a nearby metal stool, and took a seat near the door of the cage. "Good. Now let's talk about how you can control your inner wolf." He glanced at Phoebe. "This won't take long. Can you see if we can find someone to sign off on at least getting him some clothes and released from this cage?"

"I'm on it." Phoebe nodded to Leo. "Listen to Dax. He knows what he's talking about." Then she took off up the dark stairwell.

Leo's gaze stayed trained on the stairs until they both heard the door at the top slam shut. He turned to Dax. "How did you ever get a hot woman like that to share your bed?"

Dax let out a growl. "Don't ever talk about Phoebe Kilsen like she's just a piece of ass. Do you understand me?"

Even though there were bars separating them, Leo held his hands up and took a step back. "Sorry. I didn't mean any disrespect. I just meant…" He shrugged. "She's smokin' hot and smart and dangerous. That's one hell of a combination."

"Right," Dax said dryly, wondering when he'd gotten so defensive about his partner. There was no denying she could take care of herself. Hell, she could probably beat Dax's ass in a head-to-head showdown. Still, he didn't like Leo commenting on how "hot" she happened to be. She was so much more than that, and Dax knew if it hadn't been for her determination, he'd likely still be upstairs in a coma. "Now, about your inner wolf."

Leo stood perfectly still, giving Dax his full attention.

Good. He was taking this seriously. He'd need to if he wanted to get his freedom back. "You can always tell when you're going to lose control, right? Your body tenses. You're not just irritated but pissed off beyond reason. You want to literally rip someone's head off. You thirst for it like you need it to survive. Sound familiar?"

"Yeah," he said, almost in a whisper. "It's familiar."

"That's called bloodlust." Dax held the younger shifter's gaze. "It makes us no different than a vampire who feeds off the unwilling."

Leo sucked in a sharp breath, his expression stricken.

"That's right. All that hate for vampires and what they are, we have that same instinct right here." Dax pointed to his chest. "Acknowledge it. Own it. Then resolve to control it."

Leo was quiet for a moment. Then he asked the question Dax had been waiting for. "How?"

Dax nodded, pride filling him up. If he was thinking it through and asking questions, his protégé was taking this lesson seriously. "You remember who you are, who you want to be, and you embrace your human side. You hold on to the empathy that you carry with you, and you hold on tight, never forgetting that if you lose yourself to your wolf, one day, someday soon, you'll be consumed by your bloodlust."

Leo visibly shuddered in the shadows of his cage.

"And then you'll be living your life in a cell just like this one, consumed by hatred. Don't ever let go of your humanity and give others an excuse to take it from you."

"I won't," Leo said earnestly. "I promise you I won't."

Dax let Leo's words hang in the air. Then he reached his hand through the bars, offering it to the other man. The younger shifter clasped it, and the two men shook on the promise.

It wasn't long before footsteps sounded on the steps again, and Phoebe appeared with a pile of clothes and a message from the director. "No psych consult. Halston wants to see you in five."

Leo's eyes widened. "Is she coming down here?"

"Nope." Phoebe produced a set of keys. "You're being liberated."

Chapter Nine

"*D*id you tell him about the toxins in your bloodstream?" I asked Dax as we waited in the office we shared for Leo to finish his interview with the director.

Dax shook his head. "I thought it might be too much for him. I needed him to calm down and focus."

I took his hand in mine and smiled at him. "You did well. That conversation you had with him is the only reason the director decided to place him back in your custody."

Dax raised one eyebrow. "She was listening?"

"Of course," I said. "You know as well as I do that they have security cameras down there."

He nodded while I passed him the file on the eight New Orleans shifters who'd suffered an overdose in the past week. Dax opened it immediately and read Halston's directive.

"The first five are the ones we need to bring in for testing. The other three are the ones who didn't survive." I tried not to think of Rhea. "We'll need to prioritize based on the timeline of their overdoses. The ones who OD'd first need to come in ASAP. It's been six days for two of them. I'd say we could split up, but I'm not sure that's a good idea considering what happened earlier today." Not to mention, I needed to keep an eye on him and make sure he didn't turn into a rabid wolf.

"And since I no longer have a phone, that's not a good idea anyway."

I sucked in a sharp breath, suddenly remembering the text I'd gotten from him early that morning. "About that. You sent me a text this morning, and—"

"Holy shit, Phoebe! Your brother. God, I'm so sorry." Dax dropped the file on the desk and rose from his chair, quickly moving to sit on the edge of my desk. "Christ. Right after I sent that text, Leo and I got into it and my phone… Well, it died. Then I was chasing after him and the next thing I knew, I was waking up from a drug-induced coma."

I placed a light hand on his knee. "I admit I was pretty pissed to get that text and then radio silence, but I think you have a pretty good excuse. Do you mind filling me in on the details, or are you gonna make me wait another twelve hours?"

He let out a small chuckle and shook his head. "The wait is over. You know after Seth disappeared, I put a call out to a bunch of my contacts. Well, today we got a hit." He reached into the pocket where he always kept his phone and grimaced when he came up empty. "Fuck me, when am I going to remember that the phone is dead?"

I lifted both hands, palms up in an I-don't-know motion. "Care to tell me the details?"

"The address was in the text I never got to forward to you." He shook his head. "A shifter friend from Baton Rouge said he spotted him down on River Road at an old plantation. One that hasn't been turned into a tourist attraction. He was working on the house, fixing it up."

"Seriously?" I asked incredulously. "He's renovating a plantation, and that's why he disappeared on me?"

Dax shook his head. "I don't know, Phoebs. I'm just relaying the tip I received."

It was my turn to get up and pace. It made no sense why Seth was down on River Road. He was a computer hacker. A kid who spent all his days indoors, traversing the mysterious corners of the internet. Construction just wasn't part of his DNA. I shook my head. Eight years was a long time. I supposed it was possible he'd changed. Still, I wasn't convinced. "I don't think it was him. Maybe someone who looked like him, but I just don't believe it was Seth. Why would he cut all contact if he's just doing construction?"

"You're probably right. But don't you think we should at least check it out? Won't you always wonder if you don't see for yourself that it isn't him?"

He was right. That information would haunt me for years to come if I blew it off and didn't at least go take a look. "Yeah. I guess we should go. But I'm telling you right now it's a waste of time. Whoever he is, he's not Seth. And we need to find these shifters first." I gestured to the file still on his desk. "They're more important."

It was true that I was desperate to find out where my brother had gone, but I couldn't forget that Seth had left voluntarily. As far as I knew, he wasn't in any danger, unlike Dax and the shifters who were dying from Scarlet. I hadn't forgotten that Dax was quite possibly on borrowed time. I wasn't going to let anyone get in my way when it came to helping him. Not even my long-lost brother.

"Okay, we'll take a trip down there next week," he said.

Next week. After enough time had passed that Dax was no longer in danger of turning feral on us. "Sure. But right now we need to get you a new phone." I picked up the office phone and called IT. Within ten minutes, Dax had a new phone with all his preferred apps and stored contacts.

"Perfect." He slipped it into his pocket just as Leo sprinted into the room, his face flushed and excitement in his blue eyes. "Hey, man. What's got you all hyped up?" Dax asked.

"The director. She said I could assist you two this week and that if I did well, she'd consider letting me join the next recruiting class."

"Wow," I said, not at all sure what I thought of this development. Leo had been a huge help last month when we'd been in a battle with a sorceress and her demons. He'd proved to be competent and more than capable of holding his own, but after the twenty-four hours he'd had, promising him a shot at being a Void agent was a particularly bold move. "You sure you want that?"

"More than sure," Leo said, sobering. "I see what you and Dax do every day to keep this city safe, and after everything I've seen this past year, I know it's needed more than ever. I want to be part of the solution, not part of the problem."

He was so earnest my doubts all but melted away. As long as he held on to that core motivation, he'd be fine. More than fine. I glanced at Dax.

He held his hand out to Leo and said, "Congrats, kid. Here's your shot. Don't blow it."

Leo shook his hand, his expression deadly serious. "I won't. People's lives are on the line."

I stared at Leo, taking in the moment. It wasn't every day one witnessed such a transformation. Last week he'd been an eager punk kid, playing at being a shifter. Today he'd realized something important and had turned into a man right before our eyes. I just prayed the transformation was permanent, otherwise he was in for some major disappointments.

"Anyone ready for some dinner?" I asked, realizing I was starving. I couldn't even remember the last time I'd eaten.

"Absolutely," Dax said, pressing his hand to the small of my back. "Almost dying really depletes the calories."

"So does shifting and being stuffed in a cage all day," Leo added.

I glanced between them and shook my head. "Jeez, you two are delicate flowers." I grinned at them. "Buck up. At least you weren't awake for over thirty-six hours and had to babysit two different shifters all day."

Dax smirked at me.

Leo gave me a sympathetic smile and said, "You win."

I winked at him. "Come on. I'm in the mood for sushi."

Both men groaned.

I just laughed and headed out the door with both of my shifters on my heels.

~

DAX'S CLOCK read 4:57. I rolled over and stared at the ceiling. After we'd gotten back from the steakhouse they'd talked me into, I'd gone straight to bed. I'd slept eight solid hours, and was now fully awake, my brain racing.

Was it possible my brother was really only an hour away on the other side of the river? And if so, why had he disappeared into thin air? Couldn't he just take an Uber like everyone else?

It was hard to hold back the building anger toward my

brother. Eight years is a long fucking time to be gone, and then to just disappear without any explanation… I deserved better. Hot tears stung my eyes as the hollow feeling of rejection started to invade my psyche. And that just pissed me off more.

The clock ticked over to five o'clock, and I left Dax's side and headed to the shower. I turned the temperature to scalding, as if the hot water could somehow wash away my unwanted emotions. It didn't quite work that way. But as I stood there under the stream, resting my head against the cool tile, concentrating on the pain of the scalding water on my flesh, my self-confidence returned with a vengeance, and I had an overwhelming urge to kick Seth's ass.

The door hinges creaked as Dax made his way into the bathroom. Without a word, he opened the shower door and joined me. He let out a hiss as the water hit his naked body, but he didn't make a move to adjust the temperature. Instead, he encircled me from behind and bent his head to taste my shoulder.

I turned in his arms and gazed up into his dark, knowing eyes. He was no stranger to my anxiety-filled mornings, and we'd navigated this dance before. He knew exactly what I needed, and it wasn't talking.

Running a hand over his stubbled jaw, I gazed at his lips, hungry to taste him, to feel him under my fingertips, to have him take me so thoroughly that I was consumed by every inch of him.

"Kiss me," I ordered.

"I thought you'd never ask," he said gruffly and then claimed my mouth with his as he pressed me up against the wall. His already-hard cock jutted into my belly as his tongue plundered and teased and warred with mine.

Damn, he felt good. My hands roamed down his sculpted back as he grabbed my hips, pulling me tighter against him. My mind went blank, and all my worries from the past forty-eight hours vanished. All I knew was Dax and the pleasure of his touch.

That was what I needed.

Dax's hands made their way to my breasts, cupping them, then pressing them together as he tore his lips from mine and bent his head, feasting on my flesh as he made his way to one of my aching nipples. I arched back, silently begging, and let out a gasp as he scraped his teeth over the sensitive peak.

In that moment, Dax was my everything, and I wanted more. Needed to feel him inside me, claiming me.

Wrapping one leg around his hip, I slid my opposite hand down to cup his ass and jerked my hips forward, a silent message that I was more than ready.

Dax let out a strangled growl, lifted me up with both hands, and as I wrapped my legs around his waist, he took me, slammed into me, long and hard and deep.

"Yes," I whispered, holding on tight as he filled me up.

"You feel so damned good," he said, his eyes full of passion and heat as he stared down at me, holding me in place.

I pressed one hand to his cheek. "So do you. Now fuck me."

Chapter Ten

An hour later, I sat at Dax's breakfast table, completely sated as I sipped my coffee. The morning sun filtered in through the window as I leaned back and watched Dax make waffles and Leo fry the bacon.

"I could get used to this," I said.

"Which part?" Dax asked as he lifted one eyebrow and shot a glance at his bedroom door.

I chuckled. "All of it. Coffee waiting for me after my morning shower and two hot, competent men making me breakfast. What's not to like?"

Leo brought a plate of crispy bacon to the table and sat across from me. "It's a little early, don't you think?" he asked, glancing at the wall clock. "I can't remember the last time I was up before six a.m."

"No one said you had to get up." Dax placed a plate of hot waffles in front of each of us. "Though I won't complain about waking up to coffee."

"I don't think coffee is what you woke up to," Leo muttered before jamming a piece of bacon into his mouth.

Dax just laughed and took a seat.

I felt my cheeks grow warm and was almost more mortified that I was blushing than I was at the idea that Dax and I had woken Leo up with our antics in the shower.

Dax reached out and squeezed my hand while Leo smirked at me then attacked his waffles.

I cleared my throat, trying to pretend the exchange never happened. "So, we have a new case. What's the game plan for today? Any ideas?"

Leo froze with his fork midair. "Are you including me in this strategy session?"

"I don't see why not," I said as I flipped open the file the director had given me the day before. "Three heads are better than one." I wasn't sure if that was true. Leo wasn't a trained agent, but he did have a lot of contacts with supernaturals close to his age. Connections were important in our line of work, and you never knew when a source could make all the difference in the case.

He put his fork down and leaned in. "I'll do whatever you need me to."

"Damn straight you will," Dax said, then took a sip of his coffee. "We have five shifters we need to bring in to the Void. Two are our priority today. Do we want to divide and conquer or all three of us work together?"

"Divide and conquer, I think. They're both on day six, and we don't have any time to waste." I pulled out the information sheets on both of the shifters we were targeting. Now that Leo was helping us, I felt slightly more comfortable with the plan to split up. "One is a young woman, a college student who transferred to Tulane from up north. On the surface, it appears she may have just gotten caught up in the wrong crowd. The other one is a New Orleans native. He has two priors on his record, both petty theft. Works as a shift supervisor in a restaurant in the Lower Garden District."

Leo leaned over and peered at the shifter's file. "I know him."

"Really? Anything we should know?" I asked.

Dax leaned back in his chair, waiting for Leo to continue.

"Yeah. He's a small-time dealer. He's the guy social users call when they want to party."

"Interesting." I met Dax's hooded eyes, wondering if we were both thinking the same thing.

Then Dax turned to him. "Were you a customer of his?"

Leo hunched over his plate and focused on his breakfast as he grimaced and gave Dax a small nod, clearly uncomfortable answering the question. "Just a couple of times, but that was months ago and just for some extra potent pain pills, before everything went down with the Crimson Valley Pack."

"Good." Dax rested his elbows on the table and leaned forward.

Leo's head popped up, surprise radiating from his big round eyes. "Good? Did you just say good?"

Dax shrugged. "It gives us an in."

"Exactly," I agreed. "Calling him up for party favors won't raise any suspicions. You'll have an easier time making contact and, with any luck, an easier time convincing him to let the Void monitor him and any potential risks."

"Uh, okay," Leo said, sounding skeptical.

I spread a pat of butter over my waffles. "Is there something else we need to know about this guy? Did you two have any sort of falling-out, or is there any reason that he'd be wary of you?"

Leo shook his head. "No. Not that I'm aware of anyway.

What I do know is that getting him to agree to voluntarily let the Void anywhere near him is going to be a tough hill to climb. Dude doesn't trust anyone associated with the government."

"That's not a surprise," I said with a shrug. "Dealers aren't known for their cooperation. It's part of the reason we still have jobs." I sent Dax a small smile. "And bringing people in is what Dax and I specialize in. I doubt Mr...." I glanced at the sheet, "Mr. Axton has the skills to evade us. But I guess we'll find out." I turned to Dax. "How about you and Leo take on the dealer and I'll pick up the college student. Meet back at the Void by noon?"

"You got it," Dax said, a gleam in his eye as he added, "can I finish my breakfast first? I'm a little depleted after the workout this morning."

Leo snickered, and even though I wanted to say something to shut them both up, I just laughed and dug into what was left of my breakfast. Seeing Leo break through the barriers of his grief to have a moment of normalcy was worth enduring whatever they wanted to throw at me.

"Well then, eat up, boys, because we have a full day ahead of us." I raised a forkful of waffle as a toast, then tucked in.

It was still early, just past eight in the morning, when I pulled my gunmetal-gray Charger to a stop in front of a two-story, double-gallery-style house that had been broken up into individual apartments. The structure was impressive with wide white columns and wrought iron framing the lower and upper gallery porches. It wasn't exactly the type of place I expected a college student to be living. I double-checked the address for one Miss Hailee Speirs.

Yep. I was in the right place. I just hoped she hadn't already left for class. If I had to wait, it could be one hell of a long day.

I checked my appearance in the rearview mirror and was pleased with what I saw. My dark hair was pulled back into a neat ponytail. The only visible makeup was a coat of mascara and clear lip gloss. I'd opted for jeans and a T-shirt. The idea was to blend in as a college student if I had to. Plus my clothing choice would hopefully make me less intimidating. It was going to be hard enough to convince her to turn herself in to the Void for testing. I didn't want to scare her off by showing up in leather pants with a magical dagger strapped to my belt.

After shoving her file in my glove box, I pulled up my right pant leg, tucked my knife into a sheath strapped to my ankle, pulled it back down, and climbed out of the car. There was no reason to expect an altercation, but she was a shifter. Going in blind and unarmed would be unprofessional.

Just as I made my way up the stairs to the porch, the door on the far left opened and a pretty young woman rushed out. Her blond hair was piled on her head in a haphazard fashion and she wore distressed jeans with an old tank top that appeared to have a yellowish stain over her right breast. An open backpack was slung over one shoulder, revealing a load of books. She didn't even notice me as she turned to lock her front door.

"Hailee?" I asked.

She jumped, clearly startled by my voice, and half the books spilled out of her pack and scattered over the wooden porch.

I rushed over to help her gather them. "I'm sorry. I didn't mean to sneak up on you."

She waved a hand. "Don't worry about it. I just seem to be really jumpy the past few days." The shifter glanced up at me. "Do I know you?"

I handed her a biochemistry textbook and shook my head. "I doubt it. I was sent here by the Arcane."

She stiffened and froze like a deer in headlights. "Oh gods. This is about the other night at the party, isn't it? I swear on everything that is sacred that I had nothing to do with that love spell."

"Love spell?" I asked, standing and leaning against the wrought iron railing. "You mean like a potion?"

She bit her bottom lip and glanced away as her cheeks turned a faint shade of pink. "I should really learn to shut my mouth."

I chuckled. "It's all right. Really. I'm not here for that." I pulled out one of my plain business cards and handed it to her. "You're not in trouble."

"I'm not?" She stared at the card, then glanced up at me. "Phoebe Kilsen. I swear I've heard that name before."

It was possible. I'd been in the news a couple of times in the past few months. Solving high-profile cases like rescuing Allcot's consort made excellent headlines. But I wasn't one who thrived on attention, so I just shrugged and got to the point. "I'm here about the drug overdose you suffered last week."

"You're… what?" she gasped out, then covered her open mouth with her hand. "Why?"

I nodded to the small table and chairs sitting next to her front door and said, "Maybe we should sit down?"

"Yeah, maybe we should." She stared at her shaking hands.

I slipped my arm through hers and guided her the few feet to the table. "There you go," I said as I helped her into one of the chairs." Sitting across from her on the side closest to the porch stairs, I took in her pale face, the fear radiating off her, and added, "Maybe we should start over. I'm Phoebe Kilsen, a witch and a tracker for the Void. And the only reason I'm here is to help you."

She curled her fingers into a fist and said with a fair amount of defiance, "I don't need any help." Then she stood and added, "So would you please just leave me alone?"

I rose as well, blocking her path. "I'm afraid it isn't that easy. See how agitated you just got when all I did was offer help?"

"You want me to go to some religious drug treatment. I know how you people are, always thinking God can cure something. Wake up! That's not how this works." Shaking her head, she tried to make a move past me.

I intentionally let her go just to prove a point. My orders were to bring her in even if I had to force her, and I would because it was for her own sake. But I wanted to build a little trust first and see if I could get her to go willingly. "I'm not religious," I said. "And I don't think God is going to cure whatever ails you. But healers and science can help."

She paused and glanced over her shoulder at me. Frowning, she said, "I don't have a drug addiction, but thanks for your concern."

"What if I told you there is a chance that the Scarlet you took was tainted with a poison? And that drug caused a shifter to succumb to his inner wolf, resulting in the death of all his friends?"

Fear flashed in her pretty blue eyes, and I didn't miss the way her hands started to tremble again. "That's not... It can't be true."

I sighed. "Listen, Hailee, I don't want to cause you any trouble and I'm not trying to scare you. I'm trying to help you. That story really happened, and there's a real chance that you could be infected with the same poison. All I'm asking is that you come back to the Arcane facility with me so that the healers can run some tests and make sure you aren't a risk to yourself and others."

Hailee's face turned white just before her knees buckled.

Chapter Eleven

"Whoa!" I rushed to her side, catching her just before she toppled down the porch stairs.

"Oh my god." She moaned. "That's why I've been light-headed and fighting a headache the past few days, isn't it? I never get headaches. Never. And now I'm shaky and craving red meat like you can't believe." She turned to me, tears standing in her eyes. "I ate two steaks and a half-pound burger yesterday, and this morning all I've thought about is the steak tartare appetizer at the restaurant down the street. It's because I'm losing control of my wolf, isn't it?"

"We don't know that for sure. You could just have an iron deficiency." I was feeding her a line of bullshit. The headaches, the cravings, the shakes, it was likely all connected. Something was seriously off. "But we definitely need to get you to the healer just to be sure."

Tears rolled down her flushed cheeks. "I'm late for a class."

"I'm sure you can make it up." I pulled her to her feet. "Come on. Let's get going so they can start observations."

She bit her lip and glanced at her apartment. "Can I get a change of clothes? Maybe some toiletries, just in case they keep me there?"

"Sure," I said, pleased this was going so well. She seemed to understand just how serious this was. That was refreshing.

She dug in her backpack, found her keys, and while still shaking, she got the door open and led me inside.

The place looked like a tornado had rolled through it. Clothes were strewn all over the floor, a plate and matching mug were lying in the corner, both of them broken in multiple pieces. To the left, a framed poster hung askew and a hole had been punched in the wall.

"Uh, Hailee, what happened in here?" I asked, suddenly on guard.

"This!" She spun around, wielding a knife in one hand and baseball bat in the other. Her eyes glowed yellow and her teeth were bared.

"Shit!" I dodged to the right, barely avoiding getting stabbed in the shoulder. Instead, her fist came down and the blade sliced into the back of her club chair, leaving a nice long gash. "You really don't want to do this," I said, knowing I was wasting my breath trying to reason with her. She was already out of her mind and had managed to set me up by luring me inside. There was no telling how many people she'd already attacked.

She let out a growl and came for me again, this time swinging the bat at my head. I grabbed a table lamp and held it up, blocking her blow. It shattered, the ceramic pieces raining down on me while she spun, coming at me again with the bat.

It was just enough time for me to roll backward and come back up on my feet. I reached for the knife concealed at my ankle, but she came at me with her bat again, and this time she connected with my shoulder.

I was knocked to the side as pain shot straight down my arm, leaving it momentarily paralyzed. Son of a… that bitch. I blinked up at her and took in her twisted smile and gleeful expression.

"King is going to love this. Imagine his surprise when I tell him I've bagged a Void agent," she said, holding her stomach as she laughed like an evil villain in a cartoon.

"You knew who I was all along, didn't you?" I asked, trying to distract her.

She pressed the end of the bat into my chest and leaned on it. "I told you I thought you looked familiar. Once you said your name, it clicked. You're one of Allcot's bitches."

I let out a huff of incredulous laughter. "Hardly."

"Don't fuck with me," she said, crouching down to stare me in the eye. "I know all about how you saved his consort and the special arrangement you have with him. Every shifter in this town knows you work for him."

I ignored her taunts, recognizing them for what they were. Someone had trained her well. She was using basic knowledge of my past to twist it into something she knew would piss me off. But too bad for her, because I wasn't going to take the bait. I glanced at the tip of the bat still pressed into my chest and asked, "So, what are you going to do? Beat me to death?"

"No. That wouldn't be any fun." She scanned me from head to toe, her expression turning hungry. "I'm going to get that steak I've been craving. Extra rare."

My stomach turned. Was this the plan? Feed shifters Scarlet and then turn them into bloodthirsty murderers?

The bat lifted off my chest and was replaced with her foot

as she swung again, this time aiming for my head. I grabbed her ankle and twisted.

The shifter lost her balance and her momentum as she crashed to the floor beside me. I took that opportunity to retrieve my knife, and the moment she landed, I jammed it into her chest, just above her heart.

She let out a grunt of pain, and it was quickly followed by an agonized howl the second I pulled the knife out of her flesh.

"Hurts, doesn't it?" I whispered into her ear as she writhed in pain. My sunlight, which, was infused in my dagger, could kill vampires if I asked it to. In shifters, it just burned. The wound would never heal unless she found a healer willing to reverse the effects. And I was just guessing that neither Imogen nor Talisen was going to be very helpful in that regard once I got her back to the Void. At least not at first.

Normally I would've secured both her wrists with magical cuffs that would prevent her from shifting, but my last pair had been destroyed a week ago when I'd gotten into an altercation with a bitchy witch and her vampire boyfriend. They'd been shaking down a tourist when I busted them. I'd come away from the fight with most of my spelled goodies neutralized after she hit me with a particularly nasty spell. I was still rebuilding my inventory.

So, instead of securing Hailee with cuffs, I pressed my foot to her wound, making her howl in agony as she tried and failed to roll out from under me, then flipped open the top of the silver ring I wore on my right hand. Sleeping dust spilled from the chamber and rained down on her face.

"What the hell?" She threw her arms up and twisted to

the side, but it was too late. Her eyes were already closing, and her body went limp.

I stared down at her and whispered, "Sleep."

All the fight drained out of the possessed shifter as she slipped into a magically induced coma.

I let out a sigh and sank down onto the wooden coffee table. The ache in my shoulder had only intensified, and when I pressed my hand to it, I let out a sharp cry of pain. "Fuck me," I said to no one as tears stung my eyes. The shifter had really done a number on me. There was no doubt I needed a healer, and the sooner the better, but I still had a job to do. Since it was obvious I wasn't going to be able to stuff her in my car by myself while injured, I pulled out my phone and once again called Zena, my handler.

After she'd confirmed a crew was on the way, I stood and headed for the narrow hallway. As long as I was waiting for the crew, it was a good time to search her place for any clues that could help us figure out whom she was getting her drugs from. Right before I opened the door to her bedroom, I heard her phone ring and rushed back to check her screen.

Unknown caller.

Of course. I pressed the button to see if I could access her contacts, but her device was password protected. That was no surprise. Most were. That was no problem. One of the hackers back at the Void would likely be in within minutes. I slipped the phone into my pocket and made a beeline for the room at the end of the hall.

The room was immaculate, nothing like the mess she'd left in the living room. The bed was made, the dresser free of dust and clutter. And her closet looked like someone with OCD lived there. Every article of clothing was arranged by style and color.

I scanned the contents and quickly moved on to the desk that sat directly under a window. The phone in my pocket went off. And once again, Hailee's screen read unknown caller. I contemplated answering it but decided against it. I wanted the hackers to see what they could get from it first.

Her desk was just as neat as her closet. Bills were organized by vendor and date. There was a planner with every class and homework assignment listed along with days and nights to study. According to the planner, she was supposed to be at a group study session with two people, Fifi and Bird. The location wasn't listed. It just had a *K* that was circled in red.

I grabbed the planner just in case we needed to match up places she'd been or meetings she'd missed, but there was nothing else of interest. I moved on to the kitchen and was inspecting her OCD-like cabinets and drawers when I heard the front door swing open.

"Hailee, where the fuck are you? King is waiting," a male voice bellowed.

King? Who was that? And who the hell had just strolled into her apartment? I rushed back to the front of the house, wondering how I was going to spin the fact that Hailee was unconscious in the middle of her living room.

But I shouldn't have bothered worrying. The man who was crouched over her jerked his head up and growled at me, his eyes the same glowing yellow color Hailee's had been when she'd gone on the offensive.

I quickly grabbed my dagger from the sheath on my ankle and let the light flash as I brandished it in the air. "Get away from her. She needs medical attention."

He bared his teeth as his gaze locked on my blade. Then he turned his attention to the wound in her chest. He let out a bloodcurdling howl and then scooped her up and ran out the front door.

I sprinted after them, my dagger in one hand and a spell clinging to the other. I had two choices: throw my dagger and aim for his heart, or attack him with my spell and hope it was powerful enough to stop him in his tracks. I opted for the spell.

"Stop!" I cried and let my magic fly. It hit him square in the back, causing him to go down on one knee, but there was no hesitation on his part. He was back up in record time and only steps from his SUV.

Dammit. I couldn't let them get away. Hailee was too dangerous. I rushed after them and aimed. My dagger flew through the air and would've hit my target dead-on, but right at the last moment a gunshot went off, and the bullet hit the blade, shattering it and the light it carried.

My instincts kicked in and I threw myself to the ground as more shots were fired. *Bam. Bam. Bam. Bam.* All four whizzed over my head.

The sound of tires squealing drew my attention, and I glanced over just in time to see the SUV disappear around the corner. I stayed down on the grass for a few more moments, letting my heart rate return to normal and making sure the gunman was gone. There were a lot of things I could fight with magic. Bullets weren't one of them.

Neighbors from the surrounding houses started to gather in the street and chatter about what had happened. I overheard one of them say, "The gunman was in the back seat of the SUV. I saw it all go down from my front porch."

At least that answered one question. I got to my feet and ignored the pain in my shoulder as I brushed the grass off my T-shirt, then went inside and called Zena.

"They should be there in less than five minutes," she said.

"Call them off. My perp has been abducted. Shots were fired. No one was hurt, but I'm sure law enforcement is on its way. I'm going to need backup."

She let out a low whistle. "On it."

I hung up, grabbed the planner, checked to make sure I still had her phone in my pocket, and went to sit in my car and wait.

Chapter Twelve

*D*ax pulled his Trooper to a stop on Magazine Street and put the vehicle in park. He turned to Leo. "Once we get inside, I don't want you to say a word. I'll do all the talking, got it?"

"So, what? I'm the muscle?" Leo asked as he glanced out the window at the small sandwich shop.

There was an old, faded red-and-white sign that said Po'BOYS. Felix Axton, the shifter they were looking for, was the shift supervisor. Leo had called after breakfast and gotten the information after insinuating he was interested in some product.

"Something like that." Dax climbed out of the vehicle and headed toward the front door.

Leo snorted. "I think we can come up with a better plan than that, don't you?"

Dax paused and glanced back at him. He was leaning against the Trooper, his feet crossed at the ankle and his arms folded over his chest. "Okay then, what do you suggest?" he asked, just to see what the kid would say.

"How about I cover the back door and make sure he doesn't make a run for it when he sees the Void's most notorious shifter walk in? That's what I'd do if I were involved in some nefarious drug trafficking."

Dax's lips twitched with amusement. The kid had a point. "All right. You cover the back. Stop him if he cuts and runs."

"Will do, boss." Leo gave Dax a mock salute and jogged around the corner.

After he'd disappeared from sight, Dax gave Leo another few moments to get into position, then he walked into the shop.

The place was old and in serious need of a remodel. The vinyl linoleum was curling up at the edges, and the walls were gray with yellowed water stains at the ceiling. But the food case was sparkling clean, and behind the counter there didn't appear to be a crumb in sight.

A man in his midtwenties walked through the swinging door from the back of house and gave Dax a jovial, "Good afternoon. Need to order lunch?"

Dax stepped up to the counter and shook his head. "Not exactly."

Felix Axton's easygoing demeanor vanished as he took a closer look at Dax. Recognition dawned in his gaze and he scowled. "You're that shifter who turned on your pack and now you work for the Void."

"That's not how I'd describe what happened," Dax said. "But yes, I'm that shifter who works for the Void. And I have a few questions for you."

"Forget it. I don't talk to traitors who sell out their own kind." He pulled the disposable gloves off, threw them in the trash, and disappeared into the back again.

Dax shook his head, suddenly glad he had Leo along for the ride. The kid had called it. Felix's reaction wasn't a complete surprise. There were plenty of shifters in the city who hated him ever since the Crimson Valley wolf pack had been disbanded. The problem was that the events surrounding that incident were classified. Most of them had no idea that the leaders had been sacrificing fae every four years for eternal life. All they knew was that the shifters had been a respected part of the community, working to keep the place safe for people from all walks of life, and that Dax had been a part of the law enforcement team who'd brought them down for reasons unknown. To be honest, if Dax hadn't had all the details, he might be pissed too.

"Sorry, buddy," Dax heard Leo say from the back room. "You're not going anywhere until you let Marrok ask you some questions. It's official Void business."

"You set me up?" Felix asked, surprise and disgust in his tone. "You're both trash, and I'm not talking to either one of you," the man said, raising his voice.

There was a commotion, then a loud crash, and Dax heard scrambling before the pounding of footsteps as Leo yelled, "Stop!"

Dax turned on his heel, darted out the front door and around the corner just in time to see Felix heading for an eighties-model red Camaro. The tall shifter took long strides as he ran across the street, but he wasn't quick enough to outpace Dax. Just as he was climbing into his car, Dax grabbed him by the collar and dragged him back out. Once he had him on his feet, Dax twisted Felix's arm behind his back while clutching him in a choke hold.

"Going somewhere?" Dax asked him.

"Let me go, you piece of shit!" He struggled against

Dax's hold, his face turning almost purple with anger. "You have no right to touch me."

"Actually, I have every right. Because right now the Void branch of the Arcane has a directive out to bring you in. So we can either do this the easy way or the hard way."

"That's a lie. I haven't done anything," he insisted.

"Then what's this?" Leo asked, walking over to them. He had a small tin box in his hands and a scowl on his face.

Felix's gaze landed on the box, and just like that, all the fight went out of him. "Son of a…"

"What's in the tin, Leo?" Dax asked him, certain he already knew the answer.

"Red powder, a couple of needles, and stacks of cash." Leo tucked the box under his arm. "Pretty sure the director is going to have a lot of questions once she hears about this."

"Do you know what they do to low-life, drug-dealing shifters, Felix?" Dax said into the man's ear.

Felix shook his head and actually whimpered. "No."

Leo walked up to him and got in his face. Hatred rolled off him as he spoke through clenched teeth. "They put them in a cage in the basement and leave them there. Trust me when I say you don't want any part of that."

Dax was certain Leo was channeling all the pain he harbored from losing Rhea. He nodded to him, proud of the young shifter for keeping himself under control. It was because of a two-bit dealer like this asshole that he'd lost Rhea.

"I'll stop. I promise. I won't go near the stuff again. Just let me go and I'll keep my nose clean," Felix said, his voice shaking. "I can't be locked in a cage. I'll go crazy. Please. Just give me a chance."

"It's not that simple." Dax forced both of Felix's hands

behind his back. "But I'm sure concessions can be made if you answer all our questions."

"Fine. I'll tell you anything. What do you want to know?"

Dax pulled a pair of magical cuffs out of his pocket and slapped them on Felix's wrists.

"Who supplies you with the drug Scarlet?" Leo asked, getting right to the point.

The shifter's mouth worked, but he didn't spit any words out.

"Tell him," Dax ordered. "Otherwise the cell will be the least of your worries."

Sweat started to soak through Felix's T-shirt as he shook his head. "I don't... I mean, I can't say. He'll kill me."

"Well, Felix," Dax said conversationally, "today might be your lucky day."

"How so?" Felix frowned, and his brow wrinkled in confusion as he glanced at Dax. Then he took a deep breath and slowly let it out. "Please tell me I'm not going to jail."

"Oh, you're going to jail all right," Leo said as Dax jerked the shifter across the street. "It's just that you might not have to worry about your dealer killing you. He might already have set that in motion."

"What?"

"You suffered an overdose almost a week ago, correct?" Dax asked, enjoying watching Leo take command of the interrogation. The kid had the chops to be a tracker as long as he stayed focused.

"Um... yeah. But I'm totally fine now," Felix insisted. "Totally clean. I haven't used anything since that night."

"Sorry to say, but that isn't going to save you, buddy," Leo said, then explained the situation with the shifter up in

Jackson and warned him that he could be carrying the toxin that would unleash his inner wolf.

All the color drained from Felix's face. "You're saying I could be a walking time bomb?"

"That's exactly what I'm saying," Leo said, catching Dax's eye. Dax nodded, indicating for him to continue. "Now, your only option is to let Dax here take you to the Void so you can get tested. If you are carrying the toxin, you'll be staying in their care while they work on finding an antidote. If you aren't… I suppose it depends on how cooperative you are."

"Okay, okay! I get my product from a vamp named TR. He works for Cryrique. Told me his boss wanted some independent distributers. I'm just small-time, man. I swear to God. I have like four clients." He closed his eyes. "Holy shit. I have to call them, tell them not to use the shit they have."

Dax muttered a curse and tried not to think of all the shifters who might be infected with the same poison that was currently running through his veins. "Are they all shifters?"

Felix nodded.

"Give their numbers to Leo. He'll warn them for you."

"They're in the tin," he told Leo. "Please call them now. I don't want anyone to get hurt."

"And yet you sell them Scarlet," Leo said, his tone dripping with derision. "You might want to rethink your life choices, dude."

"I didn't know," he said meekly as Dax pushed him along.

"Idiot," Dax muttered under his breath as he stuffed the shifter in the back seat of his Trooper. Leo slid in next to him, already on his phone, warning Felix's clients that their stash might be tainted.

Dax jumped in the driver's seat and hightailed it to the

Void building. After watching Felix process the possibility that he'd been poisoned, Dax was more than a little anxious to find out if Talisen and Imogen had any updates on an antidote. So far, Dax had been handling the news of his possible downfall pretty well, but he suspected that was only because reality hadn't really set in yet. He was certain that if there weren't any breakthroughs, he was going to be sweating bullets just like Felix. Dax pressed his foot on the gas, tightened his grip on the wheel, and focused on the road back to the Void.

Chapter Thirteen

"What do you mean you've found nothing?" I asked Talisen as I paced his lab. "You've been working on this for two solid days. People's lives are on the line."

Talisen set his file aside and gave me a flat stare. "Do you really think Imogen and I are half-assing this?"

I stopped in my tracks and sucked in a deep breath as guilt took over. What the hell was wrong with me? "No. Sorry. I'm just frustrated by what happened today." I'd already filled him in on Hailee's condition and how we'd been too late. She was lost to the toxin. And that had really gotten under my skin. She was so young. Too young. No matter what mistakes she'd made, she didn't deserve the cards she'd been dealt.

"Did you learn anything from IT?" he asked, placing a reassuring hand on my shoulder, clearly forgiving me for snapping at him.

"Not yet." I'd dropped her phone and journal off and

was letting the experts comb through them both. "They said they'd call if they found anything of interest."

The door banged open, and Imogen walked in with Dax and Leo right behind her.

Relief flooded my system the moment I saw Dax, and it was all I could do to not rush over and wrap my arms around him. *Jesus, stop it, Phoebs*, I told myself. I couldn't do my job effectively if I was worried about Dax the entire time.

"They've got some Scarlet for us to test," Imogen said, holding up a tin box.

"And Felix Axton," Dax added. "He's in one of the exam rooms getting his blood drawn."

"Good." I opened my file and made a note next to Felix's name. The movement made my shoulder ache and I winced. I'd gotten Tal to work his magic, but he said it would still be a few days before I was back to normal. "Did he give you any trouble?"

"He did at first, but when Leo informed him he was in danger of losing control, he couldn't get in fast enough to get tested."

"That's something at least." I slumped down in a chair, still feeling defeated.

"Phoebe was too late," Talisen said softly. "Hailee has already been infected."

"Dammit!" Dax crossed the room and pulled a chair over to sit next to me. "How bad is she?"

"Is she locked in the basement?" Leo asked, his face full of concern.

I shook my head. "If only that were the case. Hailee has one hell of a swing and took a bat to my shoulder, rendering my arm useless." I ran a hand over my bruises and met Dax's worried eyes. "I'm going to be okay thanks to Tal. But after I took her out, I had to call a transport team. While I was waiting, a friend of hers showed up and hauled her out of there. I tried to stop him, but the bastard evaded me. I don't know where she is. IT has her phone. If they can hack into it, we might get some leads."

Dax didn't say a word. He didn't have to. All I needed was his presence.

"So she's just... gone?" Leo asked, his eyes wide with shock.

"Gone. There was nothing more I could do." I pulled out the handle to my dagger and waved it through the air. "I even lost my blade in the battle. Gunshots. Whoever her friends are, they weren't fucking around. She did mention someone named King. Sounded like he was the leader. Does that name ring any bells?"

Both Dax and Leo shook their heads. Phoebe glanced at Tal and Imogen, her eyebrows raised in question.

"Not that I can recall," Imogen said.

"Me neither," Tal said.

"Christ." Leo ran a hand through his hair and slowly sank into one of the chairs. "What a fucking mess."

"You can say that again." Dax turned to me. "We do have a lead on who's dealing Scarlet."

"You do?" I sat up straight, ready for some good news and ignoring the fact the director had ordered me to keep Imogen in the dark about investigating who was dealing Scarlet. If we were going to solve this, I couldn't keep any of our team in the dark. And if it turned out Imogen was feeding Allcot information, we'd find out about it anyway.

"Yep. Felix said his dealer is some vamp by the name of TR and he works for Cryrique. Supposedly he sells the drug as an independent contractor, but that part reeks of bullshit."

"Cryrique," I said, not bothering to hide my disgust. "I knew this was going to come back to Allcot. All his crap about regulating that drug and only selling to vampires was a load of shit he said to get regulation passed through government channels. Now look. Shifters are dying."

Silence settled over the room as everyone turned to look at Imogen.

"What?" she asked, taking a small step back.

"Do you know anything about Allcot's Scarlet distribution? Like who he hires to sell it or where?" I asked.

She shook her head. "No. Why would I?"

"Would you tell us if you did if it meant solving this case?" I asked, ignoring her question.

She frowned, her expression turning agitated. "Why am I here if you don't trust me?"

I shrugged. "You're an excellent healer. Just… don't take our skepticism personally. Anyone who has ties to Allcot is suspect."

"You have ties to Allcot," she said, her face flushing with anger.

I chuckled. She had a point. "True. But I don't work for him."

She stared at me for a few moments then let out a sigh. "Yes, I'd tell you if I knew anything. I don't, though. I'm just a healer who is trying to help you and the poor shifters caught in this mess."

"I'll vouch for her," Talisen said with a somber nod. "Her energy… it's pure."

That was good enough for me. Talisen could read people in a way that others couldn't. If she was lying, he'd know it. "Okay," I said then jumped out of my chair, ignoring the pain in my shoulder, and headed for the door.

"Hey, Phoebs, where are you going?" Dax asked.

"To give Eadric Allcot a piece of my mind." I turned to Talisen. "Text me when Felix's tests come in?"

"Will do." A troubled look crossed his face. "Phoebs, are you sure it's a good idea to go talk to Allcot when you're this riled up?"

"No," I said. "But I need answers, and I'm pretty sure he's the one who either has them or can get them."

"That doesn't mean he'll share them," Imogen said.

I nodded my agreement. "Don't I know it, but he owes me a giant-sized favor. I'm about to see how difficult it is to collect." Imogen and Tal both had skeptical expressions, and I could hardly blame them. Yes, it was true Allcot owed me a favor, but no one knew better than I did that all his favors came at a price and on his terms. Not mine.

"I'll go with you," Dax said. Then he turned to Leo. "Now that we're here in the lab, there's something I need to ask you."

"Yeah?" Leo crossed his arms over his chest, looking somewhat defensive. I wondered if he knew what Dax was going to ask. I had my suspicions, but I wasn't entirely sure.

"Have you ever used Scarlet?" Dax asked.

Leo blinked at his mentor. Then he shook his head. "No. Why?" His face scrunched up in disgust. "Were you afraid I shot up the same batch that killed Rhea and didn't bother to tell you even after you warned me of the problems?"

"Something like that," Dax said, now eyeing Leo with an expression that looked a lot like respect. "I just wanted to be sure, especially since you were once a customer of Felix's."

"I told you that was a long time ago for pain pills, and it was never Scarlet. So consider yourself sure." Leo cut past me and left the lab in a huff.

I met Dax's gaze. "Where's he headed?"

"To see if he can get any more information out of Felix."

"Is he going to be okay to question the shifter by himself? It's not like he's a trained investigator."

"He'll be fine," my partner said. "He's actually the one who convinced him to stop resisting and just come in and get it over with."

"Just like that? He told him he needed to get tested, so he did?" I pressed.

"Noooo, more like he scared the shit out of him by outlining his fate if he didn't. I was like a proud papa while I witnessed the exchange."

I chuckled. "Okay, sounds like he's earned his stripes for today. Let's get out of here. I'm ready to kick some vamp ass."

"Aren't you always?" Tal asked from his spot at the lab counter.

"Pretty much." I grinned at him, nodded to Imogen, then took off to find Allcot with Dax by my side.

I DROVE. The Charger purred beneath my touch as I zipped into the parking garage at the Cryrique building. It was still afternoon, and unless Allcot was out of town, I knew exactly where to find him. I even still had access to the special elevator only his elite circle was allowed to use. He'd given me a user code not long after we'd brought Pandora home. Allcot had spent weeks trying to lavish me with useless gifts from all over the world, and I'd refused them all. Then he'd come up with access. And in my line of work, that wasn't an offer I ever refused. Even though I hated pretty much everything

Allcot stood for, there definitely were times when his resources came in handy.

I was convinced that below that hard-edged shell he wore, there was still a bit of humanity lurking. There had to be. He loved fiercely and was incredibly loyal. Both were traits I admired. It was his ethics I had trouble with.

The ding of the elevator filled the silence as Dax and I exited to Allcot's private wing. The long hallway had been redone in steel, and the only door was the one at the very end of the hall. As we approached, it automatically opened. Good, Allcot knew we were there.

"Kilsen." Allcot didn't look up from his paperwork. "To what do I owe the pleasure of your company?"

"Marrok is here too, you know," I said, irritated that he was ignoring him as if Dax were beneath him.

"I'm aware." This time he did glance up and give a nod of acknowledgment to the shifter. "But I'm pretty sure you're the one driving this visit."

I ground my teeth together and had a violent urge to kick him in the balls. Instead, I stood with my arms crossed over my chest and glared. "Are you aware that the drug you manufacture for vampires is being used to poison the shifters of this town?"

He raised a skeptical eyebrow. "My company does not manufacture any pharmaceuticals that are suitable for shifters. I'm fairly certain you know this, Ms. Kilsen."

I let out a huff of irritation. "Then why is one of your employees distributing Scarlet to independent dealers around the city? Do you know who's buying that shit? Shifters. That makes you liable for overdoses and misuse."

He frowned. "Our dealers aren't supposed to sell to shifters."

"You greedy bastard," I said, so angry I could hardly see straight. "You know damned well Scarlet is being sold on the black market because you aren't doing enough to control the distribution of the product. My only question is, why? Do you not make enough profits to maintain this obnoxious fortress? Are you that big of an asshole?"

"Phoebs—" Dax started as he placed his hand on my arm.

Allcot stood and placed his hands on his desk as he leaned forward, staring me in the eye. "Ms. Kilsen, you and I have worked together before and because of that, I've afforded you leeway that I do not extend to others. If you continue to verbally attack me, then I will be forced to revoke those privileges. Are we clear?"

"I don't give a crap about your privileges," I spat out, shrugging Dax off. I knew he was just trying to keep me from burning my bridges with the vampire, but I was too pissed off to care. "Shifters are dying and going insane because someone altered your drug Scarlet. And I want to know what you're going to do about it."

Allcot didn't say anything for a moment as he appeared to take in that information. Then he glanced at Dax, probably for confirmation.

"Someone is selling a version of the drug that has a toxin in it that causes shifters to lose control of their wolf," Dax said evenly. "I think it would behoove you to know that I've been injected with this drug, and if we don't find an antidote, Phoebe has been ordered to put me out of my misery."

"I see." He turned his attention back to me. "That explains your passion at least."

He probably had a point. If Dax's life wasn't on the line,

I'd still be upset, but I wouldn't have come charging in looking for a fight. I just shrugged.

Allcot slowly sat back down. He drummed his fingers on the desk, something I wasn't sure I'd ever seen him do before. It was strange to catch him off guard without a tailor-made answer. Sitting back, he glanced up to where I stood. "What do you propose Cryrique do about this situation?"

"Are you kidding?" I asked. "Isn't it obvious? Stop manufacturing and selling Scarlet."

He nodded, and for a moment I actually thought he was going to give in to my demand. But then he said, "We could, but that horse is already out of the barn. How long do you think it would take for someone else to start flooding the market with it?"

"But Cryrique is the only corporation authorized to produce and sell it. Don't you have a patent or something?"

He shook his head and chuckled. "You think that means anything? Even if the black market didn't exist, palms will be greased and one of our competitors will be flooding the market within weeks. And there's no way to tell if they will care about regulated distribution."

"So you're saying it's better if you sell it rather than give someone else who's less *ethical* a chance to take control?" Dax asked, not bothering to hide the skepticism in his tone. "Forgive me if I don't think your motivations are one hundred percent altruistic."

Allcot's lips twitched, and I wanted to smack the smirk off his face. Unfortunately, when I considered what he'd said, I had to agree he had a fair argument. As much as I hated that the drug even existed, the fact was aside from the independent contractors, Cryrique did heavily control who had access to it. And if someone hadn't altered it and sold it to shifters, we wouldn't be having this conversation because it truly was harmless to vampires.

"I won't deny that our pharmaceuticals contribute a solid return to our bottom line, but I'm *not* in the business of killing supernaturals," he said, his tone suddenly cold. "And I resent that anyone is using our product to harm the citizens of New Orleans."

"Then why did you have your guys attack Simone?" I asked.

Allcot flicked his gaze to me, keeping his expression as cool and calculating as ever. "Simone?"

"Yeah. Simone. The swamp witch. The one I was supposed to be meeting with when Tanner attacked me."

He sat back in his chair and pressed his fingertips together. "You mean when *you* attacked my employee?"

"Goddammit, Allcot. Don't be coy. You know dammed well that Tanner was stalking and taunting me. What did you expect me to do?"

"I'd expect you to put him in his place. Which you did. I doubt he'll make that mistake again." His eyes narrowed as he added, "However, just because one of my vampires was fucking with you doesn't mean he also attacked a well-respected witch. If you find proof any such incident occurred, I would like to be informed. Until then, I'm going to assume a drifter attacked the swamp witch for reasons we'll likely never know."

Dax and I shared a confused glance. Allcot's explanation was highly out of the ordinary. It was almost as if he'd put a lot of thought into explaining away the situation. Normally he just dismissed any narrative that didn't concern him. Why was this different?

He picked up the phone and pressed a button. A second later he said, "Send Harrison in."

Harrison was a vampire on Allcot's security team. When he was still a human, he'd spent some time protecting my best friend Willow. After he decided he was ready to turn into a vamp, Allcot rewarded him for his service and turned him with no questions asked. A few months later, Willow turned him into a daywalker. I didn't know if Harrison had asked her or if Allcot had. She'd never said. But the fact was, Harrison was a good guy and I'd worked with him before.

The tall, nearly seven-foot vampire knocked once, then strode in. He was beautiful with his dark skin and onyx eyes to match. He said hello to Dax and then grinned when he saw me. "Kilsen. It's good to see you without blood splattered all over your clothes. What brings you to Allcot's office this fine afternoon?"

"Just sharing with Allcot that he's my favorite vamp," I said sarcastically.

Dax snorted and Allcot glared at me.

"She's here because someone has altered our drug Scarlet and is poisoning shifters, either trying to kill them or turn them insane," Allcot said. "I want to work with her and the Void to resolve this issue. I'd like you to be my man on the ground. Report back everything you see and hear, and I'll make some inquiries to see if we can pinpoint who's at the center of this."

"Sure thing," Harrison said.

"Is that all?" I asked.

"All?" Harrison mimicked, pressing a hand to his heart as if he'd been wounded. "And here I thought you liked me."

"She does," Dax assured him. "I think she's just expecting a little more from her favorite vamp."

I rested my fists on my hips and stared Allcot down, waiting for an answer.

"What else do you expect me to do?" he asked reasonably.

"Oh, I don't know. Maybe put your labs and vast resources to work on an antidote."

"Done." He got to his feet again and held his hand out.

I was so surprised I didn't reciprocate until Dax nudged my arm. Right. I clutched his cool hand and we shook on the agreement.

"I just need a sample to give to my researchers." Allcot leaned one hip against his desk.

"You got it," I said, pleased with our negotiations but also mildly unsettled. He'd agreed to help, but the agreement had been easy… maybe too easy. There were good reasons I didn't completely trust him. It was hard walking away not knowing if he was negotiating in good faith. Unfortunately, we were up against a deadline and I couldn't afford to turn down the one resource that could actually produce results.

Allcot's phone rang, and he dismissed us with a wave of his hand. I led the way back into the steel hallway. After the door clicked closed behind us, I turned to Dax and Harrison. "Do you think he meant it? Will he really look into the antidote?"

Dax pressed his lips into a thin line and shrugged.

"Probably," Harrison said after taking a moment to answer. Then he winked and added, "He doesn't loan out his best security detail to just anyone."

Chapter Fourteen

"It's never going to happen, Kilsen," the director said in response to my request to send Allcot a sample of the toxic Scarlet. Her blue wings fluttered in agitation as she paced back and forth in front of her desk. "Is there a reason you went to Allcot's office without informing me of your actions first?"

Yes. I'd known she wouldn't like it, but I'd needed to give him a piece of my mind. I shrugged. "I didn't think it was that big of a deal. His company manufactures that drug. He has a right to know someone is illegally altering it and distributing it."

She scowled at me. "You're making decisions above your pay grade again."

So what if I was? That wasn't new, and it was the reason I always got the job done.

"And you, Marrok," she said, turning her ire on him. "You know better."

"I think Kilsen has a point, ma'am." He stood with his feet shoulder width apart, his hands resting behind his back.

She let out an irritated huff. "This is why I detest interoffice relationships. You can't be trusted to keep each other in check."

Now that just wasn't true. If Dax went rogue, I'd take him out myself, and I knew the same was true for him. Both of us were married to the job. Not each other.

A nagging voice in the back of my mind asked, *Are you sure?*

The fact that the voice was even there was enough to tell me I wasn't. Damn. I glanced at Dax. When had that happened?

"If I had anyone else in your positions to handle this case, I'd rip it away from you so fast your heads would spin," the director was saying. "But since I don't, I have no choice other than to let you see this out. But if I hear of you going to Allcot one more time without my approval, there will be consequences. Understood?"

"Understood," Dax and I said together.

"Good. Now get back to work." She pointed to the door.

Dax started to move, but I stayed put. "Is that your final answer on letting Cryrique's scientists take a crack at the antidote for the tainted Scarlet?"

"Yes," she barked. "No is my final answer. There's no telling what Allcot and his morally compromised scientists would do with it. Our team is talented. We'll have an antidote anytime now."

I left her office shaking my head. How could she be so clueless? Allcot employed only the best and brightest. The Void? We had government workers who never seemed to stick around for the long hours and low pay.

When we were in the elevator, I turned to Dax. "If I'm going to defy a direct order, do you want to know about it?"

He pressed his hand to my lower back as he glanced down at me. His dark eyes were full of ire when he said, "Yes."

I actually took a step back, breaking our connection. "Who are you angry at? Me or the director?"

His body was so tense he looked like all it would take was one wrong word for him to lose his shit. "Not you."

I certainly couldn't blame him. The director had shut down one of the possible avenues for finding a cure for the poison still running in Dax's veins. I nodded. "Okay then. We're going to find a sample for Allcot no matter what she says."

"Damn straight we are."

I moved closer to him and wrapped my arms around his waist. Staring up at him and running my fingers over his chiseled jaw, I said, "I won't stop until you're cured. You know that, right? If I have to defy a million orders, that's what I'll do."

He sucked in a sharp breath. "I don't want you to lose your job over me."

Shaking my head, I choked out a laugh. "Do you really think I give a damn about working for the Void when politics get in the way of saving lives? You know I love my job, but I don't have to work for them to do it."

"No, but you want to."

"Not if it means losing you," I said softly. What was that I'd said about living for the job? Yeah, maybe I needed to rethink that.

The elevator came to a stop, and as the door opened, Dax slipped his hand around mine and we went to find our team.

❀

Dax and I strode into Talisen's lab. The fae was going over some notes with Imogen while Leo paced. Harrison was sitting in a folding chair, reading through a magazine. After we'd returned from Allcot's office, we'd left Harrison with them while we met with the director. Technically he wasn't working for the Void, so I hadn't had him sign an NDA. There was no doubt the director would be pissed he was present while we discussed the case, but I'd already decided I was going rogue. This case was too important. All four of them turned to us expectantly.

"How did it go?" Imogen asked.

"She's pissed," I said, slumping into a chair.

"About which part?" Talisen asked.

"All of it. She doesn't like that we talked to Allcot," I said.

"No surprise there." Talisen's green eyes flashed with irritation. "The Void has always kept everything close to the vest... even when lives are on the line."

"Well, today is no exception," I added. "She has forbidden us to give Allcot a sample of the tainted Scarlet."

Imogen put her pen down and pulled her glasses off. "But Cryrique has all the resources. If they put their best people on this, there's no telling how fast they can come up with an antidote."

"Exactly." I met Talisen's eyes and held his gaze. "That's why we're going to ignore the order."

"Good," he said without a moment's hesitation.

I grinned at him. Of all the people in the room, he was the only one I'd been worried about objecting. He'd just started working at the Void again. Defying orders could jeopardize his job. He knew that as well as I did. The fact that he cared more about saving Dax and the rest of the shifters than he did about his paycheck made me love him even more than I already did.

"There's only one problem," Imogen said. "The Scarlet you brought in with Felix is clean. Which means we don't have enough tainted product to share."

"We'll just have to find some," I said.

"How?" She was frowning as she glanced at her notes. "It's not like we can just order it online."

Dax tapped his fingers on the metal counter. "The only dealer we know about is Strix. And he's not going to sell to us."

"I know how to get it," Leo said.

The room went silent as we all turned to stare at him in question.

He shrugged. "There's a woman who hangs out at the Swamp. She sometimes sends people to him. That's why I went to her to find him. We just need someone to be the buyer. Someone he doesn't know."

"That woman wouldn't happen to go by the name Lexi, would she?" Dax asked.

Leo leaned against the counter and nodded. "You know her?"

Dax chuckled. "She's the one who tipped me off that you were looking for Strix. I have no trouble believing she sends users to him for black market Scarlet."

I glanced around the room, then nodded at Leo. "Okay, good. I'll go with you and be the undercover buyer." I turned to Dax, feeling better now that we had a plan. "While we're making our run, can you and Harrison track down the other three shifters on the list? Bring them in and get them tested."

"Sure," Dax said. "What about Felix?"

"He's clean," Imogen said. "Just like his stash."

"Good. One less shifter to worry about." I walked over to Leo and whispered, "Did he give up any more information on his supplier?" I wanted to know just how close the dealer was to Allcot. The vampire hadn't confirmed or denied using independent contractors, and I wanted proof when I took the issue to the regulatory board.

"Not yet," Leo whispered back. "He's too afraid to say anything."

"Fine," I said. "We'll just leave him in the basement and give him time to think about it."

"Dumb bastard." Leo shook his head.

"You can say that again." I turned to Harrison. "Hey, do you know a vampire named TR? Supposedly he works for Cryrique."

He glanced up from his magazine and frowned. "I don't think so." Then he shrugged. "Cryrique employs a lot of people. I can make some calls though."

"Not yet," I said. "We don't want to tip anyone off."

"Whatever you say," he said.

I nodded to Tal and Imogen. "Keep doing what you're doing. We'll be back."

"You got it, boss," Tal said while Imogen saluted and went back to studying her notes.

"Ready?" I asked the rest of them.

"Ready," they replied in unison and followed me out of the Void building. Leo and I headed toward my Charger, while Dax and Harrison crossed the street to the Trooper. The sun was low in the sky, indicating it was late afternoon. I glanced at my watch, suddenly feeling like this day had lasted a week. Time to suck it up, I told myself as I glanced over at Dax, taking in his calm yet dominating demeanor. He was my backup, the one I trusted and relied on the most. The thought of losing him to the toxin... It was unthinkable. I could sleep after we found an antidote.

"Phoebe?" Leo said.

I tore my gaze from Dax to give the young shifter my full attention. "Yeah?"

"He's going to be fine. I won't lose another person I care about."

My heart damn near exploded, and I had to fight the urge to wrap him in a giant hug. The kid was going to need to do some serious grieving when this was all over. The only way he could still be functioning at this point was by channeling all his grief into revenge. Even if he ripped the throat out of the one responsible for Rhea's death, it wasn't going to ease his pain. I knew from experience it never worked that way. But I also knew he wouldn't rest until justice was served. And maybe for now that was just what he needed.

"You're absolutely right." I climbed into the driver's seat of my car. Once Leo joined me, I turned to him and said, "This mission is a buy only. You are not to go after Strix under any circumstances. Do you understand?"

His jaw tightened, and that rage I knew he'd been suppressing rose to the surface and flashed in his eyes. "But if—"

"No." I stuffed the key in the ignition. "Not this run. This mission is to do recon and to make the purchase. That's it. Not unless I say otherwise, got it?"

His expression was pure defiance, but he didn't say anything.

"If you can't promise to control yourself, I'll make this run alone," I warned.

He shook his head. "You need me to make the contact."

I laughed. "Leo, you should know me better than that by

now." I reached into the back seat and grabbed my bag of tricks. Five minutes later, I'd turned into a blonde with bright teal streaks in my hair and fake eyelashes that made my eyes look twice as large as normal. I'd also changed into a midriff-baring halter top and stuffed my feet into four-inch bright teal heels. "What do you think?"

He stared at me with his jaw slack. Then he gave me a nod and said, "Perfect. Just the kind of barfly Strix will salivate over."

I winked and slammed the Charger into gear.

Chapter Fifteen

*L*eo led the way into the dank bar. "Another One Bites the Dust" drowned out the sound of my feet sticking to the grimy floors. Already the bar smelled of whiskey and tobacco and was packed with shifters who'd likely spent all afternoon cozied up to the barmaid.

"Classy joint," I said to Leo as I noticed a thin blonde eye him, then slide off her barstool and saunter over. Her hair was pulled up into a messy bun, her jeans threadbare, and her black bra was clearly visible through her white T-shirt.

He snorted and held his hand out to the woman as she approached. "Lexi, just the girl I was looking for."

She slipped her arm around his waist and snuggled in close while eyeing me with suspicion. "How's my favorite shifter this afternoon?"

"Better now that I've found you," he said, pulling her in for a sideways hug.

I couldn't help but wonder just how well they knew each other and if Leo had been less than forthcoming about their relationship. But then as she rested her head against his shoulder and slid her hand down to cup his ass, he grimaced and pulled away.

"I'm here on business, Lexi."

Her lower lip jutted out into an obviously practiced pout. "I'm sorry. I heard what happened to your girl, and I figured you could use some female company."

"For a hundred dollars an hour, right?" he said with one eyebrow raised.

"Well, a girl has to pay her rent." She batted her eyelashes at him.

I cleared my throat, moved to stand next to Leo, and slipped an arm through his free one. "I've got him covered."

Her frown caused deep lines around her mouth, aging her significantly.

I smiled brightly, held my hand out, and said, "Hi. I'm Karma. I heard you were the one to talk to if I wanted to score some… uh, red party favors."

She stared at my hand like it was a dead fish. "What makes you think I'm the person to talk to?"

Leo pulled his wallet out of his pocket and handed her the stack of bills he'd taken from Felix's tin. "Do you have answers now?"

She smiled sweetly, tucked the money into her black bra, and said, "Since she's here, it's going to cost you double."

Of course it was. The way this woman saw it, if it weren't for me, she'd already have Leo in a rented room upstairs and his wallet emptied as she had her way with a hot shifter.

"Sure," I said sweetly and paid her ransom.

The opportunistic barfly pulled out her phone and sent a text. The phone chimed a moment later and she said, "Head to Sinful. When you order your drink, ask for a stripper by the name of Luscious. She'll get you what you need."

"Thank you." I was already turning on my heel.

"Not so fast."

I paused. "What?"

She held her hand out. "It's another hundred for the text."

"What happens if we say no?" I asked, sort of impressed at her gumption.

"Then I'll call off the transaction as soon as you set foot out that door," she said with a shrug.

"You've got some nerve," Leo said, crossing his arms over his chest and glaring at her.

I actually chuckled to myself and handed her the money.

A grin spread across her face, transforming her into a stunning beauty as she took the cash.

Without warning, I grabbed her hand and elbow and pulled her in close to whisper, "If your tip is wrong, I'll be back and your tidy little information business is going to come to a crashing halt."

This time it was her turn to laugh. When she sobered, she eyed me with contempt. "I'd like to see you try it, sweetheart."

I gave her a knowing smile, grabbed Leo by the hand, and strolled out.

Once we were back on the street, Leo let out a low whistle. "Damn, Phoebs. You're a badass."

"You're just now noticing?" I asked with an exaggerated hair flip.

"I knew you were dangerous with a dagger, but your undercover game is off the hook," he said, shaking his head in disbelief.

"It's all part of the job." I glanced up at him. "Just think, if you follow through with working for the Void, in a year or two you could be the one wearing the halter top and four-inch heels."

His eyes flashed with humor. "If it means I'm taking down the worst in the city, then bring on the stilettos."

I chuckled. "You're okay, you know that, Leo?"

His lips curved up into a pleased smile. "Right back atcha."

We quickly made our way back to Bourbon Street, where the beer and hurricanes were flowing and tourists were already in full party mode. I quickly scanned the growing crowd then tugged Leo along and fell in line behind a woman who wore a skirt so short her ass floss was actually showing. The woman next to her had embraced a spandex jumpsuit that was so low cut I fully expected a wardrobe malfunction at any moment. Despite the fact they were commanding the attention of almost everyone within a half block, they were the perfect cover. Anyone looking in our direction would be focusing on them, not us.

Not that I expected anyone to recognize me in my barfly outfit. Still, it paid to be cautious.

It didn't take long to get to Sinful, and when I stopped across the street from the club, I told Leo to wait for me outside.

He shook his head. "No can do. Dax told me to keep an eye on you."

I rolled my eyes. "No doubt. But you're still not going in there. If anyone sees us together, it could be trouble, especially after your fight with Strix yesterday. I just want to get in and get out without any drama."

He eyed the club hungrily. "Do you think that bastard is in there?"

Yes. If this was where we were supposed to pick up the

drugs, I was certain he was in there. But I didn't want to tell Leo that. "It's hard to say. But even if he is, you're not going to touch him, right?"

Leo's nostrils flared in irritation as he clenched his fists. He sucked in a deep breath and said, "No. Not now." Then he took a step back and faded into the shadows of one of the many doorways lining the street.

"Good." I patted his arm. "I'll be right back."

The moment I started to cross the street solo, a small group of college-aged guys turned and started a round of catcalls and wolf whistles. I responded by giving them the finger.

"Bitch!" one of them yelled.

Being the classy lady that I was, I responded with double birds and slipped into Sinful. The bouncer working the door took one look at me, nodded, and waved me through as expected. Good. He hadn't recognized me. Single women almost never had to pay a cover to the strip clubs in New Orleans. But a few months ago, I'd gotten into it with a vampire inside Sinful. We'd all but trashed the place before I realized I had the wrong guy. Even though the Void paid for the damages, the owner hadn't been happy in the slightest, and I'd been banned from the establishment for the foreseeable future.

Ha. Little did they know I'd already been back three times. What can I say? I'm good at my job.

The place was one of the classiest in the city. Blue velvet covered the walls while gas lanterns hung from the ceiling, giving off a soft glow of light. I scanned the room and opted to sit at one of the tables in the shadows. A woman with long, sleek black hair was spinning around the stripper pole, her hair flying out behind her while the speakers blared "Naughty Girl" by Beyoncé.

"Hello, gorgeous," a beautiful woman I recognized as the club manager said as she sat in the chair next to me. She had flawless brown skin, wore a white silk button-down dress shirt and matching skintight trousers and had an ordering pad in one hand and a pen in the other. "What can I get for you today? Appetizers? A drink?" She scanned me, her expressive dark eyes showing interest. "Or maybe a date?" she added with a wink.

I chuckled and smiled at her, playing along with her flirting. It was unusual for the manager to wait tables, but I knew her to be aggressive with women she found attractive and that was the only reason she was at my table. She was testing me out to see if she could get my number. She wouldn't, but as long as she didn't recognize me and blow my cover, that's all I cared about. "I'll start with just a drink. Moscow Mule. And can you let Luscious know I'm here?"

"Sure thing, sweetheart. But anytime you need more than just a drink, anything at all, you know where to find me." She slid off the chair and sauntered over to the bar.

Bailey Belvins had been managing the strip club for just over a year. In all my past run-ins with her, I'd never gotten the impression that she'd allow drugs to be filtered through the club and hoped like hell she had no idea that was what was going on now. Of all the clubs in New Orleans, Sinful had seemed like the most decent one. If Bailey was in on it, that was going to be a real blow to the dancers who worked there.

Leaning back in my chair, I eyed a new dancer who took the stage. She was svelte and worked the pole like a damned Cirque du Soleil performer. Impressive.

Five minutes later, I had my Moscow Mule in my hand and my eyes glued to the incredible dancer when a sickly-sweet voice whispered in my ear, "Hi there, sexy. Ready for your lap dance?"

I glanced over at the stripper who was wearing a tiny see-through mesh skirt and a matching bra that did nothing to hide her assets. I blinked. "Lap dance?"

"Sure, sugar," she said with a purr. "You were told to ask for me, right?"

"Oh, sorry. Yes. Lap dance. I'm ready," I said, finally catching on. This was clearly all part of the transaction. I put my drink on the table just to the left of my chair and added, "Bring it on."

She giggled and ran her finger lightly down my neck. "No worries. You're not the first client to get confused. Just relax and enjoy the show. Before it's over, you'll have what you came for."

"Perfect."

I sat with my hands resting on the arms of the chair as she did a slow seductive dance, making a show of removing her top. Her breasts spilled out and she cupped them, bending in closer to give me a bird's-eye view. Then, before I knew it, she turned around and stuck her ass right in my face as she shimmied a little. Then her bottoms came off, leaving her in a barely-there bright pink G-string. When she removed her skirt, a tiny package came out of nowhere and landed in my lap. I quickly reached for it as she glanced back, winked, and put one finger to her lips. I clutched the plastic-wrapped tin and quickly shoved it into my pocket.

Luscious continued her dance, repeating many of the same moves, and when the song ended, she leaned down and kissed me on the cheek. "You'll need to pay me now for my… services."

"Right." I tucked a couple of large bills into the elastic of her G-string and added a few smaller ones for the dance. She had worked for it after all.

Her eyes glittered as she smiled at me. "Have a great night and come back and see me anytime."

"Sure." I picked up my drink and watched her strut across the club. I was just about to get up and walk out when another woman, dressed in a white fur-lined bra and panty set, appeared from the back.

Was that… *Iris*? She walked a few more feet toward the bar and stepped right into the soft glow of the light. Damn, it was Iris. Hadn't she said she was a burlesque dancer? Had that been a lie? Or did she do both?

Almost immediately, a tall, shaggy-haired vampire whom I recognized as Strix appeared behind her and grabbed her around the waist. She turned and tried to playfully swat him away, but he tightened his hold on her and bent to say something in her ear. Her expression went from amused to pissed in two seconds flat. Then they started arguing. She had her hands on her hips and was yelling at him while he towered over her. The next thing I knew, Iris had a drink in her hand and threw it right in the vampire's face. He sputtered, and his voice rose over the music as he let out a string of obscenities. He bared his fangs, and his body was vibrating with tension.

She glared at him, almost daring him to touch her again.

Strix reached for her, but the club's bouncers had arrived and were escorting him to the other side of the room. She stood back, a fierce look of determination on her face as she watched them haul Strix into a VIP area. Strix must've been a regular who spent a shit ton of money, because anyone else would've been tossed out on his ass.

I jumped up and strode over to where she was now sitting on a stool, resting her head in her hands.

"Iris?"

She jerked her head up, startled. "How do you know my name?"

I gave her a gentle smile. "I'm Phoebe. Dax's friend."

"Oh." She looked me up and down and frowned. "Why are you dressed like that?"

"It's a long story. I just saw what happened with Strix. Are you all right?"

She sucked in a sharp breath. "No. Not at all. I've never seen him react like that before."

"Are you two dating?"

"Not anymore."

Jackpot. She was the in we needed to find out more about Strix and where he was getting his stash. "Want to go somewhere and talk?"

She nodded. "I'm supposed to be dancing in a few minutes."

"I'll take care of it," I said and made my way to the end of the bar where the manager was helping the bartender mix drinks.

"Well, hello again." She gave me her full attention. "Did you change your mind about that date?"

I played along and leaned in with a smile. "I'd love to, but my boyfriend probably wouldn't like it too much."

She gave me a half shrug as she flashed a wicked grin. "It's just girls' night."

I chuckled and shook my head, amused. She was fun. "If I played for your team, I'd absolutely be interested in a girls' night. As it is, I'm pretty attached to the man and his… ah talents."

"I bet you are," she said, still smiling. "My loss. So, if it isn't a date you're looking for, what can I do for you? Another drink?"

I shook my head then gestured to Iris. "I was hoping you wouldn't mind if Iris took the rest of the night off. She's pretty shaken after what just happened with her ex, and I'd like to take her home. I think she could use a little space."

All of the amusement disappeared from Bailey's face and was replaced with disgust as she glanced at the VIP room. "I wish like hell that vampire would just stick to the other clubs he frequents. He's *always* causing trouble." She glanced back at me. "Sure. Get her out of here and I'll talk to the owner… again. The last thing I want in this club is for my girls to be harassed by dickless exes."

"Thanks," I said and squeezed her hand.

She tightened her grip on mine for a couple of beats while she held my gaze. Then she let go and winked. "If you get tired of your dude's junk, come find me. I'll make it worth your while."

I was certain she would. But as attractive as she was, she didn't have anything on Dax. "If anything changes, you'll be the first to know."

She was still chuckling over the exchange as I made my way back to Iris. Her eyes were red, but they were dry and there wasn't a tear in sight. "Okay. All cleared," I said. "Are you ready?"

"I just need to change." She slid off the stool and headed toward the employees-only door. I followed. There was no way I was letting her out of my sight. Vampires like Strix weren't known for backing down when they were pissed off.

As far as I knew, he could have found a way to slip into the back and was already waiting for her.

The small hallway was painted black and illuminated with soft red lighting. Off to the right was a small dressing room where she quickly changed into a skirt that hit at midthigh and a regular T-shirt. Except for the pounds of makeup she still had camouflaging her face, she looked just like every other coed in town.

"Okay," she said. "Where to?"

"My place." I quickly led the way back out to the street.

The moment we emerged, Leo was beside me. He opened his mouth to say something, but then his gaze landed on Iris and he promptly closed it.

"Iris is coming with us back to my place," I said. "She hasn't had the best night."

Leo twisted his head in the direction of the club, then fixed his gaze on Iris. "What were you... I mean, were you on a date or something?"

She shook her head. "Just trying to pick up some extra rent money. Things have been a little tight lately."

Both of his eyebrows shot up, and she rolled her eyes.

"It's just a job, Leo," she said sharply. "You don't need to act like I was whoring myself out. I dance. People pay me. It isn't that much different than burlesque."

Leo raised both hands. "I didn't say a word."

"You didn't have to." She turned her back to him.

Leo and I shared a glance. He shook his head and pointed back at the club then at Iris as he mouthed *Intel?*

I nodded, pleased he'd already caught on. "I'll tell you when we get to my place."

He shoved his hands in his pockets and nodded as we quickly headed back to the Charger.

Chapter Sixteen

"*H*ave a seat," I said, gesturing to the table just off the kitchen as I pulled the fridge door open. We were back at the Greek Revival townhome I shared with Willow and Tal and their wolf-shifting shih tzu, Link.

Leo and Iris both sat at the table while I reached down and picked up the small dog at my feet. He snuggled into my arms and rested his head on my shoulder, staring up at me with adoring eyes. I scratched the pup behind his ears, gave him a kiss on the head, and then set him back on the floor. He pressed his little body against my leg and waited.

"Con artist." I grabbed him a beef treat. He gobbled it down and waited for more. "Not on your life, you little moocher."

"He doesn't look like he believes you, Phoebe," Iris said, her eyes glowing with amusement as she watched Link.

"No, he doesn't. He's a spoiled little bastard." I smiled. Link and I had gotten off to a rocky start when he'd been a puppy. The little jerk had developed a taste for my shoes. The expensive ones. And oddly enough, he'd never gone after

Willow's. I was just lucky like that. But he'd redeemed himself many times over by being my backup on risky assignments. Despite his sweet fluffy-puppy persona, he was a badass wolf who'd taken down his share of vampires.

I grabbed three Mocha in Motions and brought them to the table. The drink was made by Willow, who was an earth fairy and quite talented when it came to creating magically enhanced foods and beverages. This one boosted one's energy levels. And it was safe. It wore off after a few hours and never caused anyone to go insane.

Before I sat down, I grabbed a tray of mundane muffins and put them in the middle of the table. Then I removed the wig and the false eyelashes. If I was going to convince this woman to help us, I needed to gain her trust, let her see me and not the disguise that turned me into something I wasn't.

Once I was seated, I turned to Iris. "Do you know why we were at the strip club tonight?"

"To watch the show?" she asked, tearing off a piece of a muffin.

Leo had tipped the Mocha in Motion to his lips and nearly choked at her words. "Phoebe?" he wheezed out. "Hang out at a strip club? Yeah, sure."

Beneath the table, I kicked out, jamming my pointed stiletto into his shin.

"Ouch! Son of a bitch," he muttered as he leaned down to rub his leg.

"Don't mind him," I said to Iris. "He thinks I have one foot in the grave and am entirely too uptight to go to a show."

"Aren't you though?" Leo asked, then shifted to the side to avoid another blow to his shin.

"You'd be surprised who shows up at that place," Iris said with a matter-of-fact shrug. "It's no big deal."

"It is if Phoebe is there." Leo bit into a muffin.

I rolled my eyes. He was right though. The only time I ever stepped into one of the clubs was when I was tracking a vampire or, in this instance, running down a lead on a case. The only one I wanted to watch strip these days was Dax. I shoved my hand into my pocket, pulled out the small package Luscious had dropped in my lap, and tossed it in the middle of the table.

Iris's mouth dropped open, and her eyes widened in shock. Silence filled the room as I let her take in the information.

Finally, she grabbed the small package, inspected it, then cleared her throat and asked, "How did you get this?"

I sat back in my chair, resting one hand on the table. "I bought it."

"Why?" Her eyes were narrowed and swimming with suspicion.

"Because we need to test it for toxins," Leo said, his tone clipped with impatience.

"Toxins? What?" Her head bobbed back and forth between us. "What do you mean, toxins?"

I leaned forward, staring her in the eye. "I'll tell you if you tell me everything you know about Strix's operation."

"I don't..." She closed her mouth and shook her head.

Leo pinned her with a stare. "You don't what? Don't know anything or don't want to say?"

She turned to me, her expression alarmed. "Am I in trouble here?"

I shook my head. "No. But if you withhold information, you could be." My statement was mostly a lie. Unless it was proven she was involved with the illegal trafficking of the drug, no one was going to care what a stripper knew. And while I had no interest in scaring her, time was running out. If she had the information I needed, I was going to get it one way or another.

"I'm not interested in protecting Strix," she said, venom suddenly dripping from her lips. "You did see how he treated me, didn't you?"

"I did," I said with a nod. "That's why I was hoping you'd be interested in helping us. I promise whatever you say will be confidential. There's no reason for him to know you were our informant."

"Can I get that in writing?" she asked.

I let out a huff of laughter. She was something else. "Yes, but are you sure you want that? Paper trails never seem to stay hidden in this town. Not in the information age."

Iris studied me for a moment, then nodded. "Fair point. I just don't want to end up in a cell somewhere because I dated a jackass."

"There's no chance of that if you give me what I need," I said with sincerity. "I take care of my own. You can bet on that."

She blew out a breath. "Okay then. I'll tell you what I know, but it isn't much. Strix is manipulative, secretive, and paranoid. Trust doesn't come easily with him."

"But he trusts you."

. "As much as someone like him can, I guess," she said with a shrug. "When we first started dating, I realized he was dealing Scarlet because I saw a large stash at his house along with a pile of money. He told me he only deals to vampires."

I cocked an eyebrow and tilted my head toward the stash now back in the middle of the table. "Obviously that isn't true. I was able to get this today without any trouble at all."

"The stuff Rhea"—Leo's voice broke as he said Rhea's name—"OD'd on, she got from Strix."

"That's why you tried to tear his head off at Peaches." Iris pressed her hand to her throat as tears filled her eyes. "One of the other girls told me about it."

"Yeah," he said, steel in his gaze. "I would've too if Dax hadn't been there."

Or gotten himself killed, I thought. I was certain Leo would've inflicted some serious damage on the vampire, but if Dax hadn't been there, the chances that Leo would've survived were very slim.

"That son of a bitch," she said, choking on the words. "Rhea was my friend too." Her eyes flashed with pure venom. "He knows he isn't supposed to be dealing to anyone but vampires. I swear on my life I didn't know. I never would've..." She wiped the tears from her cheeks. "I would've never been party to that."

"I believe you," I said, even as I wondered how she'd been blind to Luscious's involvement in the scheme. Iris's anger was too authentic. The dancer wasn't that good of an actress. "The question is, what are you prepared to do about it?"

"Sorry?" she asked, gazing up at me in confusion.

If I was going to track down Strix and infiltrate his operation and find out who he was working for, I needed someone on the inside. Who better than the woman Strix was still hung up on? "If I'm right and this stash of Scarlet turns out to be laced with toxins, that means Strix is one of the keys to getting to the bottom of this attack on the shifter population." I held her gaze, imploring her to understand how important she was to this operation. "Can we count on you to help us?"

She blinked rapidly. "Count on me to do what?"

Leo grabbed a muffin and leaned back in the chair. "We need you to lead us to Strix."

I sent him a pleased smile. He was acting like an old pro and had stepped in so seamlessly it was obvious Dax had already started his training to be an agent. My partner had probably been prepping him ever since Leo had played a large role in helping us take down the bastards who'd abducted Pandora last month. The Void would be lucky to get him.

Iris stood and started to pace, mumbling to herself something about being really stupid.

"Iris," I said gently, doing everything I could to hide my frustration with the fact that she seemed to be blaming herself. "Nothing Strix has done is your fault. Please don't beat yourself up about this. His actions are his own."

She froze midstep, then turned to stare at me, her expression incredulous. "My fault? Ha! Of course it isn't my fault. Strix is a jackass of the highest order. I'm frustrated because no matter how hard I try, I can't for the life of me remember where his house is."

I frowned. "What do you mean you can't remember? Did you not spend very much time there or something?"

"No. We were there all the time." She held both hands in the air, palms up. "I just have zero memory of actually going there. Or leaving, for that matter. I can tell you exactly what the house looks like, how each room is decorated, and even the pattern of his stupid dishes. I just have no recollection of how to get there or even where it is."

Leo eyed her, his brows furrowed. "Then how did you ever manage to get there?"

"He always picked me up."

"Interesting," I said, nodding. "So what did he bring you? Cookies? Chocolate? Lattes?"

"Chocolate caramels actually. How did you know that?"

"It's obvious your memory has been wiped," I said, moving to Willow's cabinet and rummaging around for her peanut butter memory bars. Once I found what I was looking for, I returned to the table and sat down. I put the three bars Willow had left in the cupboard in front of her. "He needed to get you to ingest something to make it happen. All he had to do was get the herb into you, then tell you what to forget. It works like a charm every time... unless you have something to block the active ingredient." I waved at the memory-enhancer bars.

Iris picked one up and inspected it. But then she tossed it back onto the middle of the table. "It's a moot point now. Strix and I aren't together. He's not going to come pick me up if I'm still giving him the cold shoulder."

"So stop giving him the cold shoulder," I said. "Arm yourself with the memory bar, head out there, and report back to us after you know the location. We'll take it from there."

She stared up at me with hard eyes. "You're asking me to act like I want to get back together with him."

"Yes," I said, completely unapologetic. Strix was a danger to the entire shifter population. I knew in my gut he was the reason Rhea was dead. And there was no disputing he was responsible for Dax's current predicament. There was no time for coddling. The sooner we learned who Strix's supplier was, the sooner we could bring them down.

I could go undercover and track him, but I already knew from experience that wouldn't be easy. He'd find ways to evade me, and even though I was certain that I would eventually achieve my goal, sending Iris in would be a hell of a lot faster.

"Is that all?" she asked.

"If that's all you're willing to do, then I can work with that. But if you can find out his supplier, that's the ultimate goal."

She was silent for a few beats. Then she crossed her arms over her chest, raised her chin, and said, "I'll do it."

Chapter Seventeen

"*A*re you sure you don't want backup?" I asked Iris. We were sitting in front of her house in the Charger. She was getting ready to call Strix and tell him she was ready to talk.

"Who would that be? Leo?" she asked as she glanced into the back seat where Leo had one arm draped along the back of the seat and appeared to be completely relaxed. I knew better. There was a slight vibration rolling off him, indicating that he was ready to leap at the first hint of an altercation.

"No. Not Leo," I said. "I'd call in someone who isn't emotionally attached to this case."

Leo let out a huff but didn't say anything.

"I really don't think it's a good idea," Iris said. "Strix is super paranoid about people following him. If there's even a hint of a tail, he might not even take me back to his place. It's better if I go alone. Strix is an ass, but he's never made me feel unsafe, and he's certainly never hurt me... physically anyway. That's not his style. He's more apt to try to make me jealous by sleeping with half of New Orleans instead. As long as he isn't aware his memory spell isn't working, I'm sure I'll be fine."

"He sounds like a real prize," Leo said from the back seat.

"Yeah, he hid his infidelity well. It was almost a year before I found out about his extracurricular activities." She opened the car door, and just before she hopped out, she added, "I'll call you when I get back home."

"It doesn't matter what time," I said. "And, Iris, please, just be careful. If anything feels off, you don't need to go through with this. We'll find a way."

"Don't worry. I've got this." She slammed the door.

I hated that she was going undercover for us without an agent to keep an eye on her. Though maybe… I glanced down at the ring on my left pinky. The silver band was part of the collection of jewelry that had been handed down through my grandmother. I could spell it and use it to track her later if there was a problem.

I jumped out of the car and said, "Wait a minute."

"Phoebe, really. I can handle Strix."

So naïve, I thought. Certainly she probably did have some sway over him considering they'd dated for at least a year, but if she pissed him off enough, there was no telling what the vampire might do. "I just want to bake in a layer of protection."

"How?" she asked, both hands on her hips.

"With this." I held up the ring, then whispered, "*Vestigium*." The ring glowed with my bright magic for a moment, then dulled back to its silver finish. "Wear this, and if you're gone for too long, I can track you."

She didn't reach out and take it. Instead, she tilted her head to the side and said, "You don't trust me."

Oh for the love of… "Of course I trust you. If I didn't, I

wouldn't be asking you to do this. The ring is just an added layer of protection should anything go wrong. Normally I would never send anyone out on a mission by themselves without backup. Don't you understand? This is in case the worst happens."

The suspicion drained from her expression and was replaced by surprise and something that looked a lot like fear. Good, she was finally understanding that this mission could be dangerous. She held her hand out, and I slipped the ring on her pinky finger. It fit perfectly, as if it were made for her.

"It's warm," she said.

I nodded. "It's the magic. If you feel it heating up, you'll know I'm tracking you. Got it?"

"Got it." She nodded solemnly.

"Are you still okay?" I asked her. "You don't have to do this tonight if you don't want to. You could sleep on it, make sure—"

"I'm doing it tonight," she said. "Shifter's lives are on the line, right?"

I nodded. Besides Dax, who knew who else was infected with the toxin? The sooner we figured out who was responsible for the drug, the safer the entire city would be.

"Okay then," she said with a determined nod. "Tonight it is. I'll tell Strix to come get me, and then I'll call you in the morning."

"If I don't hear from you by noon, I'll invoke the tracking spell."

"Sounds good." She turned and disappeared into the shadows of the night as she headed toward her darkened house.

I returned to the car and tried to ignore the nagging ache

149

in the pit of my stomach. As I cranked the engine, Leo slipped into the front seat.

He took one look at me and asked, "What's wrong?"

I shook my head. "I don't know. Something's off, but I don't know what."

He glanced over at the shotgun double he and Dax shared with Iris. "Do you think it was a mistake to send her into Strix's world without any backup?"

"Probably," I said with a sigh. "But I'm not sure we had a choice. She wasn't going to agree to a tail, and to be honest, I'm not convinced it would've been the best move anyway. Vamps are notoriously hard to track. If it was easy, I wouldn't have a job." I put the Charger in gear and pulled away from the curb. "I'm not even sure that's what's nagging me," I added as I turned onto Magazine Street. "It's just a feeling that something is going to go down and there's nothing I can do to stop it."

"Well," Leo said, eyeing me. "If shit is gonna go down, I can't think of anyone else I'd rather be riding shotgun with."

I glanced over at him, slightly amused. "If you keep that attitude, you're going to make a damned fine agent one day."

He didn't respond, but as he leaned back in the seat, a small smile tugged at his lips.

I FOLLOWED Leo back into the lab at the Void. The moment we stepped into the room, Dax, Talisen, and Imogen started talking at the same time. Harrison sat in a metal chair with his feet up on a desk.

"Whoa," I said. "Us first."

The three quieted down, and I handed the small package of drugs to Talisen. "We managed to score this off Strix."

"You saw that bastard?" Dax growled. He was leaning against the counter, his arms crossed over his chest. "I hope you stuck your stiletto where the sun doesn't shine."

I let out a bark of laughter. "Believe me when I say I'd have loved to. Instead, I've got someone tracking down his home residence. With any luck, we'll have it by morning, then we can storm the castle, find out who his supplier is, and bring him in for selling illegal substances."

"Really?" Dax asked. "Who?"

"Your neighbor, Iris," Leo said. "She's his ex, and he keeps sniffing around, trying to get back with her."

I quickly explained the memory-spell issue and did my best to allay their fears when all of them expressed concern about her walking right into the lion's den. "Guys, she's his ex. She knows him better than any of us. Since she was more than confident that she'd be safe, I had to take her word for it. Now, can we get back on track? We have this product to test, and I assume, since you're back, that we have shifters to question."

"Right." Imogen grabbed the Scarlet from Talisen. "I'll run a quick test to see if it's tainted with the toxin."

"Good. Use as little as possible. I want to hand over enough to Allcot so that his researchers have plenty to work with."

"You got it." She gestured to Talisen to help her and the pair put their heads down and got to work.

I turned to Dax. "Any luck on bringing in the rest of the shifters?"

"We got all three and a spare," Harrison said.

I glanced at him, then back at Dax. "A spare?"

"Yeah," Dax said, his tone weary. "We also snagged the girlfriend of one of the guys who OD'd last week. When we showed up at his door and explained he might be in danger, he got really upset and led us to his girlfriend. She was passed out in one of his spare rooms. He said she lost her shit the night before and when she wouldn't calm down, he spiked her drink with an overdose of sleeping pills."

"Let me guess. She used the same batch of Scarlet he OD'd on," I said.

Dax nodded. "She's locked up in the basement. The director has ordered tests."

"Any results yet? Are they tainted?" I asked, my entire body tense as I waited for the news.

Dax gave me a grim nod, confirming my worst fears.

A small shudder ran through me, and I had to fight to not scream. How many more shifters were out there who didn't realize they were ticking time bombs?

Imogen jerked her head up and spun around. "This is it! A hot sample."

I grimaced, ready to tear Strix's head off. It was both good news and bad news that we'd found what we were looking for. That meant the vampire was still distributing the toxic drugs. I glanced at Harrison. "Can you deliver the rest of the sample to Allcot ASAP?"

Harrison unfolded himself from his chair. "Sure."

"Imogen and Tal?"

"Yeah?" they said together.

"Can you go with him? Since you've hit a wall on finding an antidote, see if Allcot will hook you up with his researchers. Hopefully what you've discovered can help speed up the process."

Imogen nodded, but Tal hesitated.

"What is it, Tal?" I asked. "Are you having second thoughts?"

"Halston is going to be seriously pissed," he said, frowning.

"True. But in this case, I think it's probably better to ask for forgiveness than permission. Don't you?"

Everyone was silent while we waited for his answer. We all knew that if I went to the director with the request, she'd shut that idea down hard. But Imogen and Tal were getting nowhere fast. If we didn't join forces, who knew how many more shifters we'd lose?

Tal ran a hand through his auburn hair. Then he blew out a breath and nodded. "You're right." He glanced at Harrison. "Let's go before I change my mind."

Harrison nodded then led the way out the door as the other two followed.

I turned to Dax and Leo. "Should we split up? Interview the shifters you brought in separately and see if we can speed this part up?" If there was a network of dealers pushing Scarlet, we needed to know about it and shut them down as soon as possible.

"Yes. That sounds like the best plan," Dax said, already moving toward the door.

"I'll take Brian." Leo moved past Dax and quickly disappeared into the hall.

"Why does he want to interview Brian? What difference does it make?" I asked Dax. All three of the shifters were college kids who, despite being enrolled in the same school, didn't appear to have a connection to one another.

"He's the one with the girlfriend down in the basement," Dax explained. "I'm guessing Leo feels a connection since Brian's girl is in trouble."

"I see," I said, my heart aching all over again for Leo and the fact that he'd only lost Rhea a few days ago. We'd both been so focused on saving Dax, there hadn't been any time to grieve. "Do you think he can handle it?"

Dax frowned. "Honestly, I don't know. But since they have something in common, it might not be the worst idea."

"All right," I said with a nod. "Let's go see what the other two have to say, then we'll check in on Brian and Leo."

Dax opened the door for me. "After you, fearless leader."

Fearless. Right. Just about the only thing keeping me going in that moment was the overwhelming fear that I could lose Dax to the toxin in his bloodstream. *Fearless* was a crock of bullshit. I was just doing what I had to in order to make sure he didn't end up locked in a cage for the rest of his life.

Chapter Eighteen

I slipped into one of the exam rooms. A young shifter, no older than twenty, was pacing the tiled floor. The moment he spotted me, he froze. "Did the tests come back? Am I clean?"

Shit! No one had told him the news yet. I sucked in a deep breath and walked over to him, holding my hand out. "Hello, I'm Agent Kilsen. You must be Ethan."

His shoulders relaxed slightly as he clasped my hand in his and nodded. "Ethan Charles."

I squeezed his hand, then let go and gestured for him to sit down.

Panic flashed in his dark eyes. "I'm infected with the toxin, aren't I?"

"I'm afraid so," I said, holding his gaze, hoping that my calm demeanor would keep him from falling apart. I couldn't imagine what it must be like to learn you could go insane just like that while having zero hope of stopping it.

"Fuck me," he said softly. "Tanner told me that shit would

fuck me up. I guess this is the one time I should've listened to him."

"Tanner?" I sat up. "The one who works for Cryrique?"

He gritted his teeth and averted his gaze. "I shouldn't have said that."

I stood, adrenaline flooding my veins, ready to pounce. If Tanner knew Strix was selling this shit and hadn't done anything to stop him, I was going to stake his ass so hard there wouldn't even be any vampire dust to clean up. "Has Tanner been dealing this to you and your friends?"

He quickly shook his head. "No. Not at all. When he found out we were getting it from one of his runners, he put a stop to it right away. That's why we had to get it from someone else."

Tanner didn't want shifters to have the drug? That was a twist. I sat down on one of the rolling stools, piercing Ethan with my stare as I pulled out a small notebook. "Listen, I need you to be completely honest with me right now. Can you do that?"

He crossed his hands over his chest and set his lips into a grim line. "I *am* telling you the truth."

Good. There was nothing about his body language that indicated he was lying. Maybe I was finally going to get the answers I needed. "Can you confirm that Tanner is a dealer of Scarlet but that he didn't want shifters to have it?"

He nodded. "Yes."

"Okay. What about anyone else? Witches, fae, humans?"

"I can't say for sure, but I have to guess that would be a no-go too. He was very firm that he didn't want it in the wrong hands."

I scribbled down the information, wondering how Simone

had ended up with the green syringe that matched Rhea's. We knew Rhea had gotten her stash from Strix. But Tanner had been the vamp on the scene during Simone's attack. If Tanner didn't want the stuff in the wrong hands, it didn't make sense that he'd attack her with it. Or was she a user and had tried to attack him with it? There were no answers when it came to Simone. Not yet anyway. "That's good. What happened to the runner who was supplying you with the drug?"

He shrugged. "How should I know? One day he was there with the drugs, and the next week it was Tanner telling me it was over. I wouldn't be seeing another ounce. He was pissed as hell too."

"So you found another supplier?" I asked.

"Yes." He clasped his hands and started to fidget, pressing his thumbs together. He lowered his voice and in a barely audible whisper, added, "My fucking drug-addicted ass couldn't stay away."

"I'm sorry to hear that," I said, trying to hide my frustration. It didn't matter that Tanner and Cryrique had tried to do the right thing by only selling to vamps. That shit they sold was ruining lives.

"Me too," he said, sounding completely dejected.

My heart was breaking as I watched him, and as much as I wanted to reassure him in that moment that everything would turn out okay, I couldn't lie to him. And I still had a job to do. "I need to know who you went to for the new batch of Scarlet."

He stopped fidgeting and glanced away again. "I don't want to get anyone in trouble."

"Goddammit, Ethan!" I slammed my hand down on the

counter, making the young shifter jump. "People's lives are on the line, yours included. If I don't have the information I need to stop this shit from circulating through this city, more shifters are going to die or go insane."

His throat worked, but he still didn't say anything.

"There's no honor among insane shifters, Ethan," I said quietly. "Do you want whoever you're protecting to be responsible for more shifters being hurt?"

He shook his head.

"Fine. Then tell me what I need to know."

He closed his eyes for just a moment, then said, "She works at Sinful, and she goes by Luscious."

"Do you know her real name?" I asked, giving away nothing. He didn't need to know that I was already acquainted with the stripper.

"Jesus," he muttered. Then he met my gaze with an anguished look. "Mary Carol Michaels. She's a student at Tulane."

I stared him in the eye even as I scribbled in my notebook. "Did you meet her at school?"

"Yes."

I studied him, noting the sadness in his blue eyes. "Did you date her?"

"Last year. She broke up with me after she got involved with some vampire who hangs out at her club."

Strix. Of course. I wondered if Mary Carol Michaels was one of the reasons Iris had dumped his ass. Probably, as well as any number of other reasons. "Do you know where she lives?"

"Not anymore. She used to live in my dorm, but she moved out last semester."

That was no problem. I knew where to find her. I handed him my notebook. "Write down her phone number."

He scratched out a number and handed it back to me.

"Is there anything else you can think of that I should know?" I asked as I got to my feet.

"About Luscious?"

I nodded. "Or anything else you think is important."

His expression turned hard and he said, "Mary Carol isn't herself."

"How do you mean?" College girls went through a lot of changes during their four years at school. Especially if they fell into the stripper life.

"She's just... not the same. Not since she started working at that club. It's almost as if... well, as if she's being controlled."

"Why do you say that?" My skepticism was off the charts. Had he told himself that she'd dumped him because someone told her to? Was he so insecure that he just couldn't believe that she'd leave him willingly?

He let out a humorless snort. "Because, Agent Kilsen, Mary Carol broke up with me because she didn't agree with my occasional drug use. And now last week she's the one who scored some for me after my friend told me she had a contact. Does that sound like the same girl to you?"

Son of a bitch. I hadn't seen that coming. Instead of focusing on his ex, I zeroed in on the other piece of information he'd just dropped on me. "Who's your friend?"

He waved a hand. "Russ. He's in the other exam room... unless he's already gone crazy and you have him locked in a cage."

"As far as I know, he's still okay." I slipped my notebook

and pen into my pocket. "Thanks for the information. Unfortunately, you'll have to stay here until we find something to counteract the toxins in your bloodstream. Someone will be in to escort you to your accommodations shortly."

His eyes flashed amber before shifting back to their normal blue as he said, "I assume that means I'm being locked in a cage until further notice."

"No. Not unless they have to."

He let out a bark of laughter. "You mean if I lose my shit, I'm headed to the basement."

"That's exactly what I mean," I said, sympathy and irritation warring for pride of place as my dominant emotion. It sucked that his life was on hold, and I certainly didn't think he deserved to lose his mind because he was an idiot for taking Scarlet. But if he had just stayed away from the drug, he wouldn't be in this situation. None of them would. I grabbed the doorknob, pulled the door open, and slipped out into the hallway without another word. There was nothing left to say.

"Get anything?" Dax asked. He was leaning against the wall, apparently waiting for me.

I relayed the information about Tanner and Luscious.

He nodded. "Russ's story matches up. It looks like all roads lead to Strix."

"Looks like it." I quickly checked my phone, hoping for some sort of communication from Iris. Nothing. I was really starting to regret not sending a tracker with her. If Strix was more than just a small-time dealer, I'd sent her right into the lion's den like a sacrificial lamb.

"Is Felix still locked up downstairs?" I asked.

He nodded.

"Come on. I want to see what he says now that he's had time to stew in his cell. Now that we're armed with more information, that might help us shake something lose with him."

"I was thinking the same thing." Dax led the way down to the basement.

The moment we stepped into the pale light, Felix jumped to his feet. "You have to let me out of here. Drug or no drug, I'm going to go insane being locked up."

"All you need to do is tell us who you got your stash from and we'll let you go," I said.

"But I'm clean. The shit I was selling was clean," he whined. "Why does it matter?"

"Because, Felix," I said, sitting on the stool, "shifters aren't supposed to be using or selling Scarlet. We could press charges against you for dealing, but to be honest, we're more interested in who's supplying it to you so we can shut that down. But if you refuse, we'll just make an example out of you and let you rot in jail until there's room on the court docket for your case."

He closed his eyes and pressed a hand to his head. "If I out him, he'll come for me."

"What if we can provide you with some protection?" Dax asked.

I quickly shot him a what-the-hell look. He just shrugged.

"You can do that?" Felix asked, interest sparking in his dull eyes.

"Sure," I said. We *could*, but it was unlikely the agency would devote a lot of resources to such a minor player.

He let out a sigh of relief. "Good. That's good."

"But only if you're honest. No bullshit. We need names, and if you're lying, we'll add an obstruction charge to the list," I said.

He paled but nodded. "His name is TR and—"

"You already told us that," Dax said, his expression blank. "What does TR stand for?"

"I— Shit!" Felix grabbed his hair with both fists and shook his head. "I don't know, man. He just goes by TR Franklyn. He works for the vampire they call Tanner."

Dax and I shared a glance. Then I turned my attention back to Felix. "We have witness testimony that says Tanner isn't down with selling to anyone but vampires. Are you saying that's not the case?"

"No. No!" There was panic in his tone now. "I'm not saying that at all. That's exactly why I'm not supposed to out TR. He's selling the shit on the side. Don't you get it? He's skimming off the top as a side hustle. If Tanner and Allcot find out, heads will roll. TR's specifically, and mine if he gets to me before Allcot gets to him."

"TR is one of Tanner's dealers? Who's he supposed to be selling to? Random street vamps?" I asked, still confused. If they were just selling to vampires, why did they need extra dealers in the first place? Couldn't they just get it from Cryrique like the rest of the vampires in the city?

He shook his head. "No, ma'am. TR is a runner for Tanner, who makes deals with other powerful vampires. Ones not in the region, so they can distribute the shit to vamps all over the world."

And TR decided to make a little extra on the side. I nodded, finally understanding. "I see. Well, that certainly puts everything into a clearer perspective." I turned to Dax, feeling a tiny bit of the weight I'd been carrying around with me lift off my shoulders. The toxic drug and its effects were still a shit show, but I was relieved to know that Allcot wasn't purposely having his people push it to just anyone. "Tanner's guy might not be distributing toxic drugs, but he's stealing and getting shifters hooked on the stuff. Allcot will want to know ASAP."

"We'll talk to him tomorrow morning. Come on." Dax placed his hand on the small of my back. "Let's find Leo and then get some food while we wait for word from Iris."

"What about me?" Felix whined. "You said you'd let me out of here if I spilled my guts."

"We will," I said. "After we get a signed and sworn statement." I glanced at my watch. "Looks like Legal has left for the day. Maybe tomorrow if they have time."

"If they have time?" I heard him call after us as we climbed the stairs.

When we reached the brightly lit hallway, Dax started to guide me toward the exit.

I shook my head. "I can't go. I need to scour the archives for any records on Strix. There might be an address or information on his known associates. Now that Allcot and his people are cleared, Strix is our only lead. I need to devote my full attention to finding him and his lair."

"Phoebe," he said softly, "you need to eat."

"I need to find this asshole and end him before the entire city is overrun with mad shifters we have to put out of their misery." As soon as the words were out of my mouth, I wished I could stuff them back in. What the hell was wrong with me?

Dax stiffened beside me, and I wished the floor would open up and just swallow me whole. Dax didn't need to be reminded of what was waiting for him.

"I didn't mean you," I said lamely. "Besides, I'm positive Allcot won't let us down. They're probably working on a viable antidote right now."

"Of course not me." His voice was monotone and sounded far away. Then his sarcasm kicked in. "No one would ever let such a thing happen to an agent of the Void. Right, Phoebs? Void agents are far too valuable. Well, unless you factor in the politics and the posturing the directors do in order to keep their funding. But don't worry, I'm sure your boy Allcot will find an antidote just in time to save us all and will end up the hero in this Greek tragedy that never would've existed without his greedy ass in the first place."

"Dax, I—" I placed my hand on his arm, but he pulled away.

"Forget it, Phoebs." He backed up. "It is what it is. Let me know if you find anything."

I stood in the brightly lit hallway, watching as my partner stalked off, his movements stiff with anger. Just before he turned the corner, Leo quietly slipped from one of the rooms. He and Dax talked for a moment, then Leo fell into step beside his mentor and the two rounded the corner and disappeared from my sight. I let out a sigh and started to go after them, but a text came in. It was from Dax. It read: *Leo's intel from the third shifter lines up with ours. Keep looking for Strix. You're right—he's the vampire at the center of all this.*

My fingers flew rapidly over the tiny keyboard as I thanked him for the update and let him know I'd meet him back at his place just as soon as I was done in the archives.

He typed back one word: *Fine.*

My heart ached. I knew deep down he wasn't angry at me, just the situation. Hell, I would be too. Could anyone blame him? As far as any of us knew, he had five normal days left. Then what would he turn into? The thought was too painful to contemplate. I'd just have to make sure we never found out. I straightened my shoulders, held my head high, and with pure determination, I turned on my heel and made a beeline for the research department.

Chapter Nineteen

*D*ax couldn't shake the rage that was boiling within his gut. He knew none of this was Phoebe's fault. There was no reason to be angry at her, and yet Dax needed a little space. He knew she was just waiting for him to turn into some kind of a monster. He could see it in her eyes every time she looked at him. And it was all but killing him.

Maybe he should've stayed back at the Void and helped Phoebe comb through the archives, but as the day wore on, he was finding it harder and harder to focus. His blood was pounding in his ears, and sitting still was proving to be impossible. All he wanted to do was run and work out all the frustration coiling in his gut.

"You should've seen him, Dax," Leo said suddenly. The younger shifter had his hands curled so tightly into fists his knuckles had gone white. "He's barely holding it together."

"Do you think he's on the verge of losing himself to his wolf?" Dax asked as they walked across the parking garage toward his Trooper.

"No, that's not it. It's more like he's completely given up.

His girl…" Leo's voice cracked on the word *girl*. He cleared his throat. "His girl, the one he loved, is just gone. She still looks like herself in her human form, but he can't reach her. No one can. It must be pure torture. You know?"

"I can imagine," Dax said as he tried to picture Phoebe with gold eyes as she wielded her dagger with no regard for human life. A chill ran up his spine. She'd be a seriously dangerous weapon.

"At least I don't have to worry about that happening to Rhea," Leo said, venom taking over his tone. Then he glanced over at Dax and scowled. "Fuck, man. If you lose your mind… I just can't even deal with that right now."

Dax let out a derisive snort. "I'm not much a fan of the thought either."

"It won't happen to you," Leo said adamantly. "It can't. You won't let it."

Dax nodded as if he had any real control over what might happen. He'd do everything in his power to stop it, but if the toxin took him, there was nothing he could do. He couldn't outrun it. The truth was that unless Allcot's people happened to find a cure, Dax was certain he only had a handful of days left.

The thought hit him like a ton of bricks. What was he doing running off with Leo when Phoebe was back at the Void? They had assistants who could go out and get food for them. There was no reason for Dax to be taking off into the night when he should be by Phoebe's side.

He stopped in his tracks and said, "You're right, which is why we need to get back inside and help Phoebe."

"But— Argh!" Leo didn't get to finish whatever he was going to say, because right then a dark gray wolf pounced on him, knocking him to the cement.

"Fuck!" Dax shot forward, already shifting into his wolf form. His clothes ripped, and his bones broke and reformed as he morphed gracefully into a wolf. His paws hit the ground once before he leaped forward, jaws bared. But before he could reach Leo and the large gray wolf, a half-dozen wolves appeared out of nowhere, separating Leo from his sight line.

With his hackles raised, he charged forward, intending to break through, but the pack wasn't fucking around. They all closed in on him. In the next moment, he found himself in the middle of the nastiest wolf fight he'd ever been in. Jaws wrapped around his back leg as he sank his teeth into the shoulder of another wolf. Fur and teeth were everywhere.

Six on one was no match. One after another tore into him, each taking their pound of flesh with them. There was no way he was going to beat them all, but he wasn't going down without taking at least one of them with him. He eyed a pure-white wolf, and between attacks, he lunged. His teeth sank into the wolf's neck and he clamped down hard.

The other wolf let out a high-pitched cry, then went perfectly still. It was a sign of surrender, but the adrenaline pumping through Dax spurred him into action. He clamped down harder and shook his head, lifting the wolf like a rag doll, intending to shake the life out of his enemy.

He heard a faint howl behind him just before something came down hard on his back. Pain reverberated through him, and his vision turned black at the edges. His jaw went slack just as he fell to the ground, limp and unable to move.

A tall redheaded man, wearing nothing but a sneer, crouched down and stared Dax in the eye. "If Hailee doesn't wake up from her coma, I'll personally kill you with my bare hands. Got it?"

Dax blinked once.

"Good." Then the man landed a powerful kick to Dax's ribs.

Dax let out a whimper and fought to keep his eyes open as he watched the man walk over to Dax's Trooper. Red held the door open as two other naked men shoved an unconscious Leo into the back.

"Get the agent," Red ordered. "I understand he'll be one of us soon."

Dax tried to lift his head, tried to scramble to his feet, but his weary body wouldn't obey. Panic flooded his brain and his chest constricted, making it impossible to breathe. If he didn't move, he was going to be trapped in his own vehicle and taken hostage by his attackers. He had no doubt they had plenty of drugs to keep him in line. His mind raced, and he knew he had to find a way out of this situation, find a way back to Phoebe and the healers so they could help Leo. But his wounds were too great. Searing pain radiated from every open wound and at least a half-dozen broken bones. He needed a few hours minimum to heal before he'd have any chance of even crawling his way back to the Void building.

Two more of the wolves quickly shifted back into human form. Both appeared to be young, maybe college age. In unison they reached down, picked Dax up, and carried him to the Trooper. Just as they were getting ready to throw him in, Dax turned his head and clamped down on one of the shifter's hands.

"Fucking bastard!" the shifter yelled and brought his other fist down on Dax's head. The blow exploded through his already battered bones just before his world turned black.

∽

Dax woke in a room thick with humidity. Sweat coated his itchy skin, and he lay on a rough surface with no idea how long he'd been in the dark, windowless room. Hours? Days? He couldn't tell. Everything ached. He'd somehow turned back into his human form, and he was pretty sure blood coated the left side of his face and most of his body.

He tried to move, only to hear the clink of metal indicating that both his wrists and ankles were chained to something, probably a nearby wall. His first instinct was to let out a roar of frustration, to jerk on his restraints and use whatever strength he had left to free himself. But then he heard the callous voices floating in from a neighboring room.

"What the hell are we going to do with the grandpa in the pit? That dude is old as fuck," someone with a high-pitched voice said with a snicker. If Dax had to guess, he'd say the voice belonged to a kid, probably in his teens.

There was a rustling sound. Then someone sniffed and in a gruff voice said, "Like it or not, he's one of us now."

"Don't you always say you can't teach old dogs new tricks?" the kid asked. "Even if he can be brought over, it's going to take forever. How is that worth it?"

"If we'd left him with that bitch of a witch, there's no telling what she would've done with him," Gruff said. "Imagine what she could turn him into right after the drug kicks in."

"Jesus. You're right," the kid said, his tone hushed now. "Nightmare."

"Now imagine if he breaks and we turn him into one of us. Think of what we can make him do to his bitch." Gruff let out a sinister laugh. "She'll wish she were dead."

Dax sucked in a labored breath. They were talking as if they were going to turn him into some sort of sadistic robot who would do their bidding. Was that what they were doing with the rest of the shifters? No wonder they were all young. They were still impressionable and easier to control.

"The blond kid, now he's a damned good score," Gruff said. "He's got the skills we're looking for. Real leader, that one."

"I won't work for that punk ass," the kid scoffed. "That little bitch bit me. I bet I have rabies now."

"He's a wolf, not a fucking raccoon. And you'll do whatever I fucking tell you to, Boomer. Or would you prefer I throw your ass in one of the pits while you readjust your attitude?"

"Fuck you, Cade," Boomer said. "King's in charge around here, not you."

There was a commotion followed by a loud grunt. Then Dax heard Gruff let out a growl before he said, "You heard King. When he's not here, you do what I tell you to. Got it?"

Boomer grunted.

"What was that? I didn't hear you."

"Yes, sir," Boomer squeaked out.

"That's right, soldier." There was another rustling, then the sound of a chair scraping against a wood floor. "Next time you get the urge to talk back to your commanding officer, you won't just be nursing a fucking welt on your head, I'll give you a goddamned broken arm. Understood?"

"Yes, sir," Boomer said again.

"Good. Now go get the little bitch in room two. We need to have a chat."

Footsteps echoed off the walls, followed by silence. Dax tried to put their conversation in some sort of context. Sir. Commanding officer. Training shifters... It didn't take a genius to figure out these pieces of shit were building some sort of army. But for what?

More footsteps sounded from the other room along with some sort of struggle that resulted in things crashing to the floor.

"Put him on the table," Gruff said.

There was a grunt then a loud thud. "This bastard is heavier than he looks."

"Wake him up."

"Why? Can't we just pump him full of Scarlet while he's out? Seems a hell of a lot easier."

"Shit," Dax muttered under his breath and involuntarily yanked on his chains.

"Sounds like Grandpa's awake," Boomer said.

The door squeaked as it swung open, and light splashed into the barren room. Dax flinched and recoiled from the bright light.

"You look like shit," Boomer said.

"He looks like he got his ass kicked," Cade said.

Dax opened his eyes just in time to see a boot come right at his face. He heard the crunch of his nose just before pain exploded through his skull and his lights went out again.

Chapter Twenty

I'd been sitting at the research computer for so long my eyes were starting to cross. The vampire Strix had over two dozen addresses. Each one had proved to be either an empty lot, a strip club, or a blood bar on Basin. I'd worked my way through all his known associates and had only come up with three viable addresses, all of them small apartments that didn't match the large place Iris had described. I'd even searched for anyone who went by King in an effort to follow up on Hailee's lead but came up with absolutely no one in New Orleans.

The only shifter I found who went by King was one who was based in the UK and worked in security for a vampire organization that was as large and powerful as Cryrique. According to the travel information, he hadn't even been in the States for over twenty years. It was highly unlikely he had anything to do with the toxic Scarlet.

I sat back in my chair, rubbed my eyes, and then squinted at the clock. Holy hell, had I really been at it for two hours? I picked up my phone to check for messages. None. Dax still hadn't called or texted. Neither had Leo, not that I'd expected him to. But Dax… I'd figured he'd call after he had a chance to cool off. I quickly tapped out a text asking if he'd gone home after picking up food.

No immediate response.

I tucked the phone into my pocket and decided he must've crashed for the night. It was just after midnight. And if I didn't want to be dead on my feet the next day, I was going to need to get some sleep as well. The only question was where? My place or his?

Normally the answer was obvious. We hadn't spent a night apart in over a month, and I'd told him I'd meet him there. Even so, after him giving me the cold shoulder, I was tempted to go home to my own bed. To give him the space he needed to come to terms with his new reality. He didn't need me pointing out the obvious while I vented about the case. I knew I wouldn't though. I'd show up on his doorstep sooner or later. The truth was I couldn't deny the pull that had me already deciding I needed to see him, to know he was okay. Because I knew from experience that Dax never slept through a phone call or text notice. Shifters were light sleepers, and unless he really was ignoring me, he hadn't gotten my text.

The more I thought about it, the more anxious I became. Dax was not sleeping. Something was seriously wrong. With my phone in one hand and the keys to the Charger in the other, I tore out of the research lab and hauled ass to the parking garage. In less than two minutes, I was in my Charger and tearing out of the garage.

Then I saw it. It was just a glimpse of fabric, but it was fabric I knew well. The same silver-blue shirt Dax had been wearing earlier that day. I slammed on the brakes and jumped out of the car. I found the shirt first and pressed it to my nose, taking in Dax's familiar woodsy smell. As I glanced around, I spotted his jeans and boots and underclothes.

Trepidation mixed with real fear made my heart speed up. "Son of a bitch!" Dax never left his clothes just lying around after an unexpected shift unless he ended up tracking someone. But he'd left over two hours ago. Wouldn't he have called if he'd run into trouble?

There was also the fact that Dax hadn't answered my text. That meant one of two things: he either didn't have his phone or he was physically unable to call me. I grabbed his jeans and checked the pockets. Nothing. No keys. No phone. I supposed it was possible Leo had grabbed his keys and was driving, but if Dax had his phone, why wasn't he answering?

I quickly tapped out a 911 text, telling him it was urgent he contact me.

A faint beep came from under one of the nearby cars.

My heart caught in my throat. I immediately pulled up Dax's name and hit Call. The ringing came from my left. I followed it until I fished the phone out, then shone a light under the cars, looking for his keys.

They were nowhere.

Panicked, I called Leo. It went straight to voicemail. After sending a text that went unanswered, I grabbed Dax's phone and ran back into the Void building.

"I thought you were headed home for the night," the guard called after me as I sprinted past him.

I didn't answer as I made a beeline for the stairs. Two flights later and I stood inside the tech lab, breathing heavily as I handed the phone to the tech on duty.

She glanced at it and frowned. "Looks like one of ours. What's it need?"

I sucked in air and huffed out, "Break through the password. I need access."

She handed it back. "You know I can't do that. Not with company phones. It's against protocol."

I thrust it back into her hands. "Daxon Marrok is missing. I have a strong suspicion so is his Trooper. I happen to know he keeps a tracking app for his vehicle on this phone. If I can get into it, I can track him down before he loses his mind and turns into a monster no one can control. Now, are you going to help me, or do I need to get the director on the phone?"

"I can't—"

"Forget it." I hit the director's private number.

Almost immediately, the woman's voice barked in my ear. "This had better be important."

"I need you to authorize a phone hack. It's Dax's and—"

"You know that's against protocol, Kilsen."

"That's why I'm calling you," I snapped, no longer giving a shit about pissing someone off. They were both wasting time. "Dax is missing, and I have reason to believe there's foul play involved. But more importantly, we've been separated, and if the toxin hits him when I'm not around—"

"Give the phone to the tech," she ordered.

I did as I was told and waited for the director to give the order.

The tech nodded and said, "Yes ma'am. I will, ma'am." Then she handed the phone back to me. "She wants to talk to you again."

Of course she did. I was well prepared for the ass chewing. I wasn't supposed to let Dax out of my sight, and yet I hadn't even thought to go after him when he'd snapped at me and then stalked off.

"Thank you, Director," I said into the phone.

"Don't thank me yet. Once you find him, bring him straight back to the Void. He's not to be out in the general public until this matter is resolved. Do you understand?"

"But—"

"I don't want to hear it, Kilsen. I had one condition, and you broke it. Marrok is dangerous. Bring him in or there will be consequences."

"Yes ma'am," I said, only to realize a second later that she'd already ended the call. "Fuck," I muttered under my breath.

"You can say that again." The tech connected the phone to her computer with a USB cable, and her fingers flew over the keyboard as she tapped her program that killed the security features on his government-issued phone. "Whatever Marrok did, he's in deep shit."

"You have no idea," I said.

A moment later, she handed me the phone. "It's an open book now, so don't let it land in the wrong hands."

"I won't. Thanks." Without another word, I spun on my heel and sprinted back to the parking lot. The moment I slid back into my Charger, I activated the tracking device on his phone.

A map of New Orleans popped up on the screen. A blue dot indicating the location of the phone appeared, followed by a thin blue line that led out of the city. But when the line reached the edge of the bayou, it stopped mapping and a spinning wheel appeared on the screen.

I waited and waited and waited, and still the wheel continued to spin.

"Dammit!" I wanted to throw the phone, smash it against something, but instead I tucked it into the console and laid my foot on the gas. I'd just have to pray the app started to work again or else I was going to hit a dead end out in the bayou.

I couldn't recall ever pushing the Charger as hard as I did that night. During the straightaway on the freeway, the speedometer topped 140. If not for the two other cars on the road, it's possible I'd have pushed it to the limit. But even I wasn't that crazy.

In no time, I crossed the line into the back roads of the bayou, only to have the app blink out on the phone. I gritted my teeth and pulled over into a gravel parking lot in front of a broken-down shack that had an impeccable sign that read: GATORS, BAIT, AND HURRICANES.

I tapped the icon of the tracking app on the phone. Nothing happened. I tapped it again, got it to flash up on the screen, but it closed immediately. After a few more tries, I cursed and tossed Dax's phone into the passenger's seat. There was clearly something in the area interfering with the technology.

"Now what?" I said out loud to nobody. I couldn't just go back into town. Dax was out here somewhere. But if I just started driving around, not only would my chances of finding him be next to zero, if I did manage to stumble upon him, my element of surprise would be nonexistent. And if he was in trouble, all I'd manage to do would be to get myself ambushed before I could be of any assistance. I had to find him another way.

The orange moon was high in the sky, casting an eerie glow over the bayou. I stared up at it and started to feel a tingle of energy wash over my skin. It was faint, but it was there.

Magic. It was in the air, it permeated it, and it was likely what was blocking the technology I needed to find Dax's

Trooper. Someone had cast a spell over the entire area. Gooseflesh popped up on my skin. Whoever had cast the spell was powerful, perhaps more powerful than I was. There was only one way to find out, and that was to fight magic with magic.

I pushed my door open and uncurled from the protection of my vehicle. Once I was outside, the magic was more noticeable. It brushed against my skin and made the hair stand up on the back of my neck. It was thick and ugly and meant to harm. There was no question I should've had backup in this situation, but my sense of urgency was off the charts. If Dax was out there, I had to find him, and soon.

Standing with my hands over my head, I stretched my arms out toward the moon and called up my magic. The familiar warmth started in the pit of my stomach and spread through my limbs, instantly calming me. I pictured Dax's handsome face in my mind and opened my heart, letting all my emotions for him free. Love and trust and bonds of friendship overwhelmed me, bringing tears to my eyes.

I blinked and barely noticed when the tears rolled down my face. All I saw was Dax's dark eyes and the love that reflected back at me every time we shared ourselves with one another. My skin tingled with the memory of his touch, and my heart skipped a beat as I recalled his gentle kisses. Then I focused on his wolf and his fierce protectiveness. All my memories of him collided, swirling in a collage of chaos, making my head spin.

"Dax," I whispered and was gratified when my magic responded. The chaos stopped, and clear as day, I saw Dax standing in front of me, naked as if he'd just transformed into his human form. I smiled at him and said, "Show me."

He shook his head in defeat.

I frowned. "Just show me where you are."

He waved a hand, opening a window into his world. All I saw was a dark room with Dax lying naked on a wood floor. His hands and feet were chained to rings that were screwed into the wall. There was nothing to show me where he was or how to get there. Disappointment crashed into me and I took a step back, rocked by my failure.

Dax turned back to me with regret in his eyes. It was as if he was admitting defeat.

"No!" I cried. "You will not give up. You hear me? You will fight this, fight them, and you will stay alive and sane until I find you. Understand?"

He shook his head again, this time a flash of pity flickering in his gaze.

"Daxon Marrok, don't you fucking dare." I pointed my finger at him, waving it in his face. "I will find you, and you will not turn into some crazy monster. Get it through your thick skull right now. Phoebe Kilsen does *not* lose. You will still be the same Dax as you were last week, the Dax I know and love, when I find your sorry ass. Don't give up on me now, because I sure as hell haven't given up on you."

The pity and defeat had vanished. This time when his gaze met mine, I was rewarded with fierce determination. Then he nodded and disappeared into thin air.

Chapter Twenty-One

*D*ax woke with a start. Phoebe's face was swimming in his mind, and one word stuck with him. *Survive.*

Phoebe was out there, and she was coming, he was sure of it. All he had to do was stay alive and keep Leo from being infected with the toxin.

A small sliver of light shone through the tiny crack between the barely open door and the frame. It was enough to show him that he was still chained to the wall. But at least this time when he moved his arms, the pain was dulled, indicating he was healing. It also meant there was a strong possibility he could shift his way out of his restraints.

The most common way to keep a shifter locked up was to drug them with a substance that would keep them from shifting. But thanks to Phoebe's magic and the five-pointed pentacle she'd convinced him to let her tattoo into his skin, he was immune to that particular substance.

Dax sucked in a deep breath and braced himself. After the beating he'd taken, the sane thing to do was to wait at least forty-eight hours before trying to shift. But Dax didn't have any time to waste. If he was going to protect Leo, it was now or never.

In the next room, his captors were still having a heavy debate on whether to wake Leo or not. One thought they shouldn't. He was ready to drug Leo right then and there. Another argued they needed to be more careful, make sure they didn't kill him with an overdose. She said he was too pretty to die. Another thought they should wait for King. Others agreed, then a loud argument broke out. Dax didn't really care about the particulars. He just knew he needed to be free and ready to fight for the kid.

Every muscle already ached. Every bone felt bruised and battered. Weariness seeped deep inside every cell. His entire being begged for sleep, for healing, for nourishment. He ignored it all and went to the quiet place in his mind where he pictured himself shifting into his wolf.

The dark gray image of himself sauntered out into his mind, and in the next moment, excruciating pain made him bite down hard on his tongue to keep himself from crying out. Thousands upon thousands of sharp needles stabbed into every inch of his skin while his bones felt as if they were disintegrating inside his body. His entire world was one deep pool of torture.

He wasn't even sure he had the energy to survive the shift, and he had a moment of wondering if he'd ever wake from his hell or if he'd just descend to the fiery gates for eternity. He'd never much believed in heaven and hell, but in that moment, he was a believer and he knew his place. Dax had spent much of his life pretending he was one of the good guys. But he knew now he was a beast, just like every other wolf and vampire out there. A beast who deserved what he got, deserved to suffer. Deserved to live forever in the nasty underworld with no joy, no sunshine, and most of all, no compassion.

Then his paws scraped the floor. The cloud of despair lifted, taking his delusional dreams with it. Dax blinked. The dark room came into focus, and he was relieved to realize no one was watching over him.

The voices from the next room rose as the argument turned from injecting Leo with the toxic Scarlet to locking him up in chains. Dax paused, contemplating his next move. If he walked out into the other room in wolf form, there was no telling how they would react. He could only do that if he planned on physically attacking them. With Leo unconscious, he'd be no help, and Dax had already seen the ramifications of a fight that was six to one. Who knew how many other shifters were holed up in the broken-down shack? He'd have to do this another way.

Standing there in the dark, Dax once again focused and kept his jaws clamped tight so as not to howl out the pain. Though this time his shift wasn't as horrible as the last. Good. That meant he was healing. Within seconds, he was standing barefoot on the rough floor. He didn't even bother to look for clothes. He already knew there weren't any. If they'd wanted him dressed, they'd have clothed him before they shackled him to the wall.

His footsteps were silent as he made his way to the door. He had to take a moment to let his eyes adjust to the harsh light. Once the room came into focus, he blinked a few times, not at all sure his mind wasn't playing tricks on him.

The room was bathed in red velvet—the walls, settees, and armchairs. Gold accents were everywhere from the arms of the chairs to the tassels on the curtains to the table off to the left where Leo was lying on his stomach, his bare ass mooning the entire room. The group had disappeared and all that remained was a young shifter with dark black hair, barely twenty years old, who sat with his legs draped over one of the ornate gold arms of a red velvet armchair. And another one who appeared a few years older was standing by a pair of french doors, smoking a cigarette while he stared at Leo with a hunger in his eyes. Not blood hunger. No, that was pure lust.

Dax's stomach rolled. Not because the shifter appeared to be interested in men but because the guy was turned on by an unconscious person with wounds marring his body, most likely inflicted by him. Dax cleared his throat.

The kid scrambled to stand up and instead ended up flailing right out of the chair. The smoker turned and stared at Dax, sweeping his gaze over him and lingering at Dax's hips.

"Nice cock," he said, his voice gruff. "Too bad you won't get to fuck your woman with it ever again."

Cade, Dax thought. He recognized the voice. Dax registered the man's words but understood them for what they were. Cade was just trying to throw Dax off guard, get under his skin to make sure he had the upper hand should this confrontation turn to violence. Dax wasn't taking the bait.

"I bet you'd like to get your hands on it though, right, Cade?" the younger one said with a snicker as he got to his feet. "If Grandpa here was a little younger, he'd be just your type. Big, dumb, and too pretty for his own good."

"Shut your fucking mouth, Boomer," Cade ordered. "No one asked for your commentary."

"What did you do to Leo?" Dax asked, ignoring their exchange.

Cade shrugged one shoulder. "The usual. A few blows here and there until he passed out."

"No different than a Friday night at the queer bar, eh, Cade?" Boomer said under his breath.

Cade moved with lightning speed and brought his fist down so hard on the younger shifter's cheekbone Dax was surprised it didn't shatter.

Boomer let out a roar, then scrambled to his feet as two of his teeth fell to the carpet. He clamped his hand over his mouth and mumbled, "You fucked up my teeth, you piece of shit."

"Don't ever talk about my sexual preference again, got it, asshole?" Cade ordered as he glared down at the other shifter.

"Jesus, psycho. I was just fucking around," Boomer said.

Cade grabbed him by the shoulders, roughly spun him around, and then kicked him in the ass and said, "Get the fuck out of here. And don't come back unless you're summoned."

Boomer scurried from the room, leaving Dax and Leo alone with Cade.

Cade waved a hand toward a pair of armchairs. "Have a seat, Agent Marrok."

Dax glanced once at Leo, then back at Cade. The shifter was wearing ripped jeans, a tight black button-down shirt, and pristine white tennis shoes that looked like he'd just pulled them out of the box.

"Please. I'm intensely interested in how you managed to escape your shackles," Cade said.

No shit, Dax thought. But he'd be damned if he told the other shifter anything unless Dax got something out of it. "Wake Leo first, and then I'll tell you."

Cade chuckled as he shook his head. "Can't. The drug will wear off soon enough. Until then, let's talk."

Dax's gaze darted from Leo to the french doors and then to the door across the room that led into the rest of the house.

Cade sat in one of the chairs and rested one ankle over the opposite knee. "You can try it, but I guarantee you won't get far. The place is crawling with King's pack, most of them crazier than an outhouse rat."

King. That was Hailee's leader. Well, Dax thought, at least he'd definitely found ground zero. One way or another, he was going to find out exactly what was going on with the toxic Scarlet and the poisoning of New Orleans's shifters. Dax sat down in the chair, leaned back, and mimicked Cade's relaxed sitting position.

Cade's eyes gleamed with interest. "Good. I can see you're a man who can be reasoned with. You just might be the shifter we've needed all along."

"For what?" Dax asked.

Cade snorted. "I'm the one asking questions. Not you."

"If you want me to answer, there has to be a give and take," Dax said and lifted one shoulder in a half-hearted shrug.

"That's fair," another man said from behind them.

Dax glanced over his shoulder and had to work to keep his rage in check. It was Red, the shifter who'd put his lights out back at the Void building.

Cade jumped up from his chair and waved for the other man to sit. Once Red was settled, Cade asked, "Can I get you anything, sir? Water? Bourbon? Whiskey?"

"Two steaks. Rare. Have Hailee bring us two bourbons on the rocks," Red said without even looking at Cade.

Hailee. She must've woken from Phoebe's spell.

"Yes, sir." Cade said, sounding completely different from the cocky asshole who'd just been sitting across from Dax.

Red gave his minion a condescending smile, then turned to Dax. "Good evening, Agent Marrok. I see you've already met some of my pack. Eager bunch, aren't they?"

"Your pack?" Dax asked. "I assume that means you're King."

"You catch on quickly." He snapped his fingers, and instantly a small blond woman hurried into the room.

"Yes, sir?"

"Please bring Mr. Marrok some fresh clothes. Jeans and a T-shirt. No shoes." He turned his attention back to Dax. "Don't want you to think you're free to just walk out of here."

Dax let out a bark of laughter. "I wouldn't dream of it."

"Right."

Within moments, Dax was clothed and had a bourbon in his hand. He raised his drink and took a good long look at the amber liquid. "Want to tell me what this seduction is all about?" he asked King. "You already have me here. As far as I know, I'm infected with the toxin that turns shifters insane. Looks like you hold all the cards in this poker game."

"Maybe I just want your cooperation."

"For what?" Dax asked.

"The coming war with Allcot and his bullshit company," King said without hesitation.

Dax blinked. "Is that what all this is about? A shifter-vampire war? What do you hope to gain? Looks like you have all the money you could possibly need."

King snorted. "You think this is mine?" He stood and walked around the room, gesturing to the gaudy furniture and ostentatious artwork. Dax hadn't taken a good look at the paintings before, but now that King had pointed them out, he studied them and noted that each and every one depicted vampires biting women while shifters guarded their masters.

"This place belongs to a vampire," Dax said. It wasn't a question, but King answered anyway.

"I think you know him." He waved a hand and Strix walked in with Iris at his side. She was wearing a see-through lace teddy and matching robe that did very little to cover any part of her. She had her arm around his waist and was leaning into him with her head resting on his chest while he caressed her bare arm. There wasn't any part of her that looked like she wasn't exactly where she wanted to be.

Had Iris played Phoebe? Had she been in on Strix's game all along? Dax quickly glanced at her left hand and spotted the silver ring. Relief rushed through him. If Iris hadn't wanted Phoebe to find her, then surely she would've taken the ring off before she let Strix pick her up. Maybe she was a better actress than any one of them had given her credit for.

"Iris?" Dax asked, letting surprise fill his tone. Strix would know that Dax was her neighbor and that they knew each other. "What the hell are you doing here with this asshole?"

She shrugged and glanced up at Strix, giving him a flirty little smile. "What can I say? He's my kryptonite. I just can't seem to stay away."

"That's right, baby," he said and leaned down to nudge her neck. She tilted her head to the side, giving him full access to her throat. His fangs descended, and Iris shivered as he scraped them down her flesh and over her pulse.

"Save it for the bedroom." King's face scrunched up in disgust.

"It's been a minute," Strix said. "Right, baby?" He trailed a finger over Iris's breast.

Her smile fell for just a second, and that one tell clued Dax in on the fact she wasn't enjoying being manhandled by the vampire. His suspicion that she might not have been telling Phoebe the whole truth fled. She was the real deal, and he knew he could count on her when the time came. Suddenly their odds were looking a little better.

"Right, baby," she mimicked but then slipped her hand over his and removed it from her bare flesh. "Still, we don't want to make anyone uncomfortable."

"Fuck that. It's my goddamned house." Strix glared at King. "I'll do whatever I fucking want."

King stared him down. The room was completely silent as the two men glared at each other. Finally Strix held his hands up and took a step back. "Fine. No PDA. Got it. If you losers would find some pussy, maybe you wouldn't be so uptight all the time."

"Strix," Iris chided. "Don't be crass."

He leered at her. "But you like my dirty mouth when we're in the bedroom."

Iris flushed deep red and shook her head as she strode out of the room. Strix followed her, practically salivating.

"Charming," Dax said to King after the door slammed behind them. "That's who you have working on your team? All it's gonna take is one girl who gets under his skin and he's gonna fuck everything up." Little did King know that one girl was already on the inside.

"You think I don't know that?" King asked. "Why do you think I brought you here?"

Dax shrugged one shoulder. "To clean up his mess?"

He laughed. "Mess? Ha! You're the one thing he did right. With you on our side, Glacier has the potential to go head-to-head with Cryrique in the corporate world. And

Eadric Allcot's power will be cut off where it hurts him most
—his bank account."

"So that's what this is about? You want Cryrique's market
share? Of what, Scarlet?"

His lips curled into a slow, predatory smile. "All of it.
Scarlet, the magic-infused pharmaceuticals, gene therapy for
vampires and shifters, weight loss supplements, cosmetics,
synthetic blood. You name it, we'll produce and distribute it."

"And where does the shifter army come in?" Dax asked.

"Protection. Security. Right now Glacier can't compete
with Cryrique. They have far too many daywalkers. Too
many strength-enhancing drugs. Do you know what they do
to competitors?"

Dax could guess. Cryrique didn't stand for anyone getting
in their way. Not on the streets and not in business. "I
imagine Allcot sends his goons and one way or another,
whoever was working on the latest project either ends up
working for Cryrique or ends up missing. How'd I do?"

"Just about right on the nose." King lifted his glass in a
salute. "And that's why we want you on our team."

"Do I have a choice?" Dax asked, swallowing the
resentment threatening to choke him.

"Everyone has a choice," King said. "You can either
choose to be with us or against us. If you're with us, you'll be
free to live your life as you see fit. If you're against us... I
guess we'll have to figure out a better way to keep you
chained up."

"Some choice," Dax said and picked up the bourbon.
He'd yet to take a drink, but he did press the glass to his lips
and sniff the liquid. As far as he could tell, it wasn't tainted.
Still, he wouldn't risk it. Just because it smelled fine didn't
mean it hadn't been magically altered.

"It's not a bad life." King rose from his chair. "Once the team is in place, the boss man will set everyone up with their own houses, cars, staff. You'll have everything you need. No more working for the corrupt government and their bullshit salary. You'll basically be doing the same job, only on your own terms."

"You mean Glacier's terms."

He laughed. "This is why I like you, Marrok. No bullshit gets by you. Think of what we could build together."

"What if I say yes?" he asked. "What happens when this shit in my veins starts to take over?"

He waved an unconcerned hand. "It's just like a steroid, meant to build your physical strength. Once it kicks in, you go through some training, learn to control it, and come out the other side stronger and faster than you ever imagined."

"Have you taken it?" Dax asked, watching him carefully.

"Yes," he said without hesitation. Then he locked eyes with Dax. His green eyes flashed pure gold as he added, "I was the first."

Dax nodded, pretending to contemplate the other shifter's offer. Then he asked, "How long does it take to go through conditioning? And do I get to build my own team?"

"Conditioning usually lasts a couple days to a few weeks after the toxin activates in your bloodstream. It all depends on what kind of control you have. Someone like you, I'd guess a day or two tops." He pursed his lips as he studied Dax. "As for building your own team, you'll have to prove yourself first."

"After that, this magical life of riches and prestige just appears out of nowhere?"

"Not nowhere, Marrok. It's funded by Paul Macer, owner of Glacier's parent company Macer, Inc."

"Holy shit," Dax muttered. Now it all made sense. Paul Macer was the richest vampire in Europe, the natural rival to Allcot and his company Cryrique. There had been reports some six months back that there'd been a deal to join forces so that Cryrique had a presence in Europe while Macer had one in the US. Only the deal fell apart when Allcot partnered with the Barrés, a vampire dynasty from the northeast that was rapidly moving into the UK markets. Was Macer so crazy that this was some sort of revenge?

"Exactly," King said as he pulled his wallet out of his pocket. He quickly flipped it open and showed Dax a picture of a mini-mansion on the side of a hill overlooking the bluest sea he'd ever seen. "This is my place in Greece. I have another one in Italy and a condo in Paris. All you have to do is play ball and by this time next year, Macer will set you up anywhere you want to be."

Sure, Dax thought. All you have to do is play ball. Dax glanced up and gave the other shifter a cocky grin, pretending interest in his fancy houses and bullshit status. Nothing ever came without a price. And Dax wasn't willing to bargain his life or his integrity for some house on the side of a mountain. But before he showed his hand, he needed to get Leo the hell out.

"I'm in," Dax said. "But I want Leo on my team. The kid is like a son to me. That's a deal breaker if I can't have him."

"Why do you think we brought him here?" King stood and moved to the gold table.

Dax followed him and watched as the shifter pulled out a syringe.

King held the syringe out to Dax and said, "He's yours if you have the balls to make him one of us."

Chapter Twenty-Two

ake Leo one of them? King was out of his goddamned mind if he thought Dax was going to inject that shit into anyone, let alone Leo. But he had to play along if he had any hope of saving the kid from that very fate. Dax took the syringe, mostly just to get it out of King's hands. No one was going to inject Leo with that toxic shit if Dax had anything to say about it.

"Go on." He gestured to Leo's arm. "The sooner you get on with it, the sooner you'll be set up in your mansion on a hill."

Jesus, this guy must've thought Dax was the shallowest fucker on the planet. Was a house all it took to ruin another guy's life? Dax leaned over Leo's prone form.

The moment his face was shielded from King's view, Leo opened his eyes and mouthed, *No!*

Good, he was awake. That would make this easier. Dax gave him the tiniest shake of his head, indicating he had no intention of injecting the drug into Leo's bloodstream. Then he bent his head and pushed up the sleeve of Leo's T-shirt, exposing the kid's shoulder as he whispered, "Keep your arm close to your body. Got it?"

Leo mouthed, *Yes*.

"Whatever happens, just pretend you're high. Trust me," Dax said, his voice so low he wasn't even sure Leo heard him.

"How much do I give him?" Dax asked, holding the syringe so that the needle was straight up. He pressed the plunger, sending a tiny spray of the red liquid in the air.

"Don't waste it, man. That shit is precious," King said, running a hand through his thick red hair. "Expensive too."

"Sorry." Dax gave King an apologetic smile. "Old medic training."

King's eyebrows shot up. "Military?"

Dax nodded. "Six years. It sticks with you."

"Nice. That'll come in handy." He nodded to the syringe in Dax's hand. "It's already prepped. Give him all of it unless he's never shot up before."

"Leo isn't a user." Dax gripped Leo's arm, holding the younger shifter steady. "I've never seen him high before."

"In that case, give him half and you take the other half," King ordered.

"Why? I don't want to be high," Dax said. "That's not my bag."

"Too fucking bad, Agent." King strode up to Dax and got in his face. "No one knows exactly how much of the toxin got into your system. We need to know that you're one of us, and the only way to do that is to make sure you've got enough of the drug in your bloodstream. Understand?"

Dax understood perfectly. They were making him prove himself twice before they decided to trust him. Well, joke was on them. Leo wasn't getting a drop of their shit. Not if Dax had anything to say about it. "Fine. Care to step back so I can get to work?"

"Yeah, I mind. This is something I have to see," he said with a gleeful laugh.

Fucker, Dax thought. Fine. If he wanted to watch, he was going to get one hell of a show. Dax quickly undid the button and zipper of his jeans, then yanked the denim down, exposing his hip. Without any fanfare, Dax jabbed the needle into the fleshy part of his upper thigh and let out a grunt. He pressed the plunger of the syringe and hissed as the vile drug worked its way into his bloodstream.

Instantly the drug went to Dax's head and his vision blurred.

"Jesus fucking Christ!" King roared as Dax spun and faced the small blurry crowd that had gathered at the far door. "Look at this guy. His balls are bigger than mine."

In Dax's already fuzzy state, he briefly wondered if King meant his actual balls. Dax glanced down to see his jeans had fallen to his ankles, and King was bent over, cackling at the scene.

Now! The voice sounded in Dax's head. Do it now. Dax turned, grabbed Leo's upper arm, and aimed. By some miracle, the needle hit the fleshy part of his own thumb just as he intended. He stared down at Leo and through clenched teeth said, "Hiss as if it hurts like a motherfucker."

Leo sucked in a sharp breath, grunted, and then threw Dax off him. The syringe went flying through the air. Dax watched it, his vision blurred and his body feeling as if it were weightless. Then he heard Leo say, "Fuckin' A, man. This shit is amazing."

Dax floated in and out of awareness. He knew he hadn't passed out; he just couldn't remember what was going on around him. Leo was there. So were King and Strix and Iris. Their faces peered down at him, King's and Strix's amused, Leo's and Iris's worried. He tried to tell them he was fine, but his tongue was too thick and wouldn't let him get the words out.

Eventually he became aware he was in a large bed, sandwiched between Leo and Iris. Iris was mopping his head with a cool rag. Leo was stretched out, pretending to sleep off his high. But the moment Dax moved, they both sat straight up.

"Jesus, Dax. You okay, man?" Leo asked.

"I have no idea," Dax croaked out. "Water?"

Iris reached for a cup on her side of the bed and handed it to him. Dax gratefully gulped the water down. As soon as he emptied the cup, he glanced up at Iris and asked, "That wasn't laced with anything was it?"

She shook her head. "Not that I know of."

"Good." He closed his eyes and took a deep breath. "Are you both all right?"

"Yeah," they said in unison.

Dax glanced between the two of them, noting the stress lining their lips and the dark smudges under their eyes. "What is it?"

"Nothing," Iris said, fierce determination shining from her light eyes.

"Doesn't sound like nothing."

"She thinks Strix is on to her," Leo said quietly.

"Why?"

"Because I wouldn't sleep with his sleazy ass," she ground out. "I told him it's because I'm still trying to learn to trust him, but he doesn't believe me. The moment I volunteered to keep an eye on you both, he knew. I'm pretty sure I'm never getting out of this room."

"Of course you are," Dax said, sitting up. His head was fuzzy from the drugs and his limbs ached from his still-healing wounds, but at least he could think. "I'll get you both out of here, one way or another."

"I've been telling her that, but she's not convinced." Leo placed his hand on Dax's arm. "Hey, thanks, man. What you did for me back there... I don't even know what to say. You saved my ass."

"You don't have to say anything," Dax said. "My blood is already tainted by the toxin. Taking more isn't going to change anything."

"It was still really fucking heroic," Iris said.

Dax patted her hand and slipped out of the bed. Iris quickly glanced away, her cheeks turning bright red. He looked down at himself and realized he was once again completely naked. "What happened to my clothes?"

"You ripped them off during your rendition of 'Love Shack,'" Leo said with a snicker.

Dax eyed him, trying to determine if the kid was fucking with him. But then Iris and Leo caught each other's gazes and both of them burst out with the lyrics of the chorus, and Dax knew he'd never live down the shame. "Christ," he muttered.

Leo and Iris both laughed.

"Don't worry," Iris said. "I got it on video, so you can watch it later."

"Great." He shook his head and moved to the window. The orange moon was still high in the sky. "How long was I out?"

"A couple of hours," Leo said. "Apparently your

metabolism is faster than most, even for a shifter. They said we'd be out of it for hours."

Dax saw his opening. "So they aren't expecting us to emerge anytime soon?"

Iris shook her head. "Not until morning. Though who knows when Strix will come looking for me again." Her nose wrinkled in disgust as she added, "He just never gives up."

Dax moved to an armoire and pulled out fresh clothes. Just like every other shifter compound he'd ever been in, there were clothes stashed everywhere. Once he was in another pair of jeans and a T-shirt, he glanced back at the two still sitting on the bed. "What kind of resources do we have? Any vehicles we can snag? Weapons? Elements of surprise?"

"The only vehicle I've seen is Strix's. It's in the garage, but it's impossible to steal. And even if you did, he'd track it down in no time flat. The man has at least half a dozen trackers on that thing," Iris said.

Of course he did. Dax would too if he drove a Bugatti. "Weapons?"

"I found this." Leo pulled a small steak knife out from under the pillow.

Dax raised one eyebrow.

"What? It's a knife. Got any better ideas?" he asked defensively.

"Yeah. How about we just walk right the fuck out of here?" Dax turned to Iris. "Any idea where we are?"

She nodded, a grin spreading across her face. "Sure do, thanks to Phoebe." Her smile vanished and was replaced with a scowl. "Unfortunately, we're on a small island out in the fucking bayou."

"Strix got his fucking Bugatti out here?" Leo asked incredulously.

"It's a private car ferry. Only runs for him. The rest of us get a foot bridge that looks like one wrong step will put us in the swamp."

"Great," Dax said. "Well, it's now or never. You in?"

She jumped off the bed. Leo followed, but just as they were about to slip through the french doors, he hesitated.

"What is it?" Dax asked him.

"Do we have all the information we need to bring them down? You know the minute we walk out of here, they'll find a new place to hole up."

Dax grinned, pleased by the kid's commitment. "Thanks to King, I've got everything we need to put the pieces together. Once the Void finds out, the shit is gonna hit the fan."

Leo let out a sigh of relief. "Good. Then let's get the fuck out of here."

Dax held the door open for them, but the minute he stepped out into the humid air, he let out a long string of curses.

King stood in the middle of a dozen shifters. They were all lined up, just waiting for the trio to try to make an escape. King stepped forward, his arms crossed over his chest. "You didn't think we believed that shit show, did you?"

Dax shrugged. "It was worth a shot."

"Let's hope you think so while you're down in the pit with the rats."

"Rats?" Iris squeaked out, taking a step closer to Leo. The younger shifter put his arm around her, holding her protectively to his side.

"Get your fucking mutt hands off her," Strix said from behind them.

Iris spun, and before anyone else could move, Strix struck, hitting her so hard across the face that the impact was followed by her gut-wrenching cry echoing across the bayou.

"You piece of shit!" Leo lunged, shifting instantly, going for the vampire's throat. Dax was right behind him. His jaws locked on Strix's wrist, and with savage rage running straight from his core, he clamped down and shook his head, intending to rip the limb right off. No one assaulted a woman in front of Dax and got away with it... especially not Strix.

The rest of the wolves shifted, and just like what had happened in the parking garage, it was once again two against far too many. Claws and jaws were everywhere. Fur flew, flesh ripped, bones were broken. No one was giving up, and Dax was prepared to fight to the bitter end. But then something strange happened. A blanket of magic fell over them, making it feel as if they were moving through molasses. The fight came to a complete stop as Strix and each of the shifters tried to get out from under the heavy magic to see who had arrived.

Phoebe, Dax thought. She must've found them.

But then he heard Iris whisper in his ear. "The ring is getting hot. I just have to keep it up until she gets here."

"Keep what up?" Dax asked her, searching the crowd for Leo. He finally found his protégé lying in a patch of mud, trying to pry another shifter's jaws from his arm.

"The magic. I just have to keep it up until Phoebe gets here."

She showed Dax her silver ring. It was glowing.

Agent Kilsen was most definitely on her way. And if Dax knew her, she was bringing the cavalry with her.

Dax tore his gaze from the ring to Iris's pale face. She was already sweating and starting to tremble from the effort she was exerting.

Shit! She was going to lose it any minute.

"Iris, how long have you been practicing magic?" he asked.

"Oh, about five minutes," she huffed out. "Phoebe said I had the gift, but... Well, all I did was try to stop the fight so you two could escape and now..." She sucked in a labored breath. "Here we are."

"Whoa. Okay." Dax held out his hands to her. "Take them in yours."

She did as he said.

"Good. That's very good." He watched as her trembling stopped and some of the color came back into her face. "Perfect. Just like that. Channel my energy. It's all good."

Dax's eyes started to get heavy, and he knew Iris was tapping every last bit of his energy, but he was not giving up. If she could use him to keep the shifters from tearing their throats out, then so be it. He'd give everything he had and more. Because Phoebe was coming.

Chapter Twenty-Three

*A*fter the tracker for finding Dax's Trooper failed me and he hadn't been able to tell me where he was once I contacted him through my magic, I only had one more trick up my sleeve. I just prayed that wherever Iris was, Dax and Leo were nearby. But first I needed reinforcements. I could take on a vampire. That was no problem, but if Strix had an entourage of other vamps or crazy shifters, I was going to need help.

I could've called the Void and had them send me security and backup, but I couldn't be sure the director wouldn't call me in and make me get any plan to invade Strix's residence approved before I went ahead with the operation. And after contacting Dax, it was clear he was in trouble. Waiting wasn't an option.

Instead, I called Pandora. I could've called Allcot, but I wanted someone to say yes with no questions asked. After last month, Pandora had made it clear that if I ever needed anything, she was only one phone call away. And where Pandora went, Allcot was sure to follow.

"Kilsen? It's four in the morning. What's going on?" she asked.

"I need an army. Now. Dax and Leo are in trouble."

There was a small pause on the other end of the line. Then she said, "Where are you?"

I rattled off the cross streets and the name of the small shack in the gravel parking lot.

"We'll be there in ten." The line went dead.

A cool breeze flittered over my skin, and for the first time that night, I felt as if things were finally going my way. I tucked my phone into my back pocket and got to work.

The pentacle-shaped pendant that had once belonged to my grandmother was nestled against my chest, the silver cool to the touch. But the minute I closed my fist around it, pictured Iris in my mind, and whispered, "*Vestigium,*" Iris's energy washed over me and I saw her standing outside, her face pale and her body trembling from effort. She was bathed in magic, too much magic, magic that would drain her dry.

My heart raced and sweat coated my skin as I felt every bit of her struggle. She was fighting for her life, for the lives of others, for the lives of Dax and Leo. My heart nearly burst out of my chest. They were all together, and Iris was all but sacrificing herself for them.

"Son of a... Hold on, Iris," I said. "I'm coming. I promise."

Phoebe's coming. I heard her words in my mind.

Then Dax was right there in front of her, holding her hands, lending her his strength.

I let out a breath as the scene vanished from my mind. My heart ached, and my insides felt hollowed out. Three people I cared very deeply about were barely holding on, and I was stuck in a holding pattern.

"Hurry!" I shouted into the night. Then, as if I'd actually summoned them, Pandora, Allcot, and five other of his loyal vampires dropped right out of the sky.

"You summoned?" Pandora said. Her long blond hair was piled up into a messy but elegant bun. She wore stylish jeans, a bright red fringe shirt, and spiked heels. Allcot also wore jeans, a red shirt, and cowboy boots.

I blinked, unable to process their cowboy and cowgirl outfits. "What—"

"It was roll-playing night," she said with an amused smile. "It never hurts to spice things up a little."

Allcot cleared his throat. "As much as I enjoy talking about our sex life, maybe we can come back to this later." He turned to me. "Don't we have shifters to save?"

"Yes." I wrapped my hand around the pendant again and closed my eyes. An image of a compass flashed in my mind, pointing in the direction of my ring. "Southeast. That's where they are."

Without another word, Allcot wrapped an arm around my waist and took off, flying into the night. I should've been pissed considering he hadn't even warned me, but honestly this was the fastest mode of transportation. The compass in my head steered us directly to where we wanted to go.

I pointed down, indicating they were right below us.

Pandora raised her hand, then when she dropped it, they all descended as one, landing in a circle that surrounded the shifters.

"Oh my god!" Iris exclaimed. Her magic vanished with her utter shock, and suddenly the shifters were on their feet, all of them going straight for Dax, who had used all his energy to help Iris keep them subdued. He had fallen to his knees and was breathing heavily, trying to get his strength back. Two shifters were already on him, tearing at his already battered flesh, when I reached his side.

Magic crackled at my fingertips, but I didn't want to unleash it, knowing it might hit Dax. Instead, I pounced as if I were one of the vampires and clamped my hands around the woman's neck… the woman I recognized as Hailee.

She kicked and bucked and threw her head back, but I was strong. Stronger than her, even in her souped-up state. Stronger because my magic was fueling my adrenaline, feeding off my rage.

"Don't ever touch him again, Hailee," I said as I poured magic into her, lighting her up and zapping her shifter energy. "If you do, my magic will be the least of your worries."

Without waiting for an answer, I threw her against the wall of the house. Her body slammed so hard against the old wood siding that the nearby window shattered. I grinned.

Another shifter pounced, landing on Dax. His golden-red fur shone in the moonlight. But instead of lunging for me, he shifted into his human form, turning into a well-built redhead who oozed confidence and charm. He held out his hand. "You must be Phoebe Kilsen."

I stared at his hand but didn't take it. "And you are?"

"My people just call me King."

"They call you a thief and a vampire killer," Allcot said from behind me. His tone was conversational, but he wasn't fooling me. Allcot hated this bastard. I could tell by his overly polite tone. Allcot never talked like that to anyone except his mortal enemies right before he ended them.

"Eadric," King said, "why am I not surprised to see you here? You always did have a soft spot for the difficult ladies, didn't you?"

"He's here because of me," Pandora said, appearing out

of the darkness, her hair down and flying behind her like some warrior princess.

"Pandora." King's hatred rolled off him in waves as he glared at her. "Are you planning on breaking my neck again? Or maybe this time you'll just go ahead and rip my heart out and stomp on it with your fucking heels. I'm sure it will feel just about the same."

"Fuck you, King. You were the one who left me for dead, remember?" She shared a glance with Allcot. "If Eadric hadn't come along, well, it's possible you would've spent the rest of your sorry days on death row. So maybe you owe him a thank-you."

"I see you all know each other," I said sarcastically. Of course they did. I eyed King. "Was all this just some sort of revenge plot all along? Why involve innocent shifters?"

"Drug-addicted shifters aren't innocent, Kilsen," he spat out.

"They are when you're the one who's forcing drugs into their veins," a shrill voice called. Then the stripper I knew as Luscious ran up behind him and buried a knife deep in his back.

The shifter let out a howl and sank to his knees.

Pandora laughed. Allcot shook his head. I stared at Luscious, who was backing up, shaking her head, tears rolling down her cheeks. Good goddess, she was a human. I hadn't been trying to identify her species status when I'd met her at the strip club, and after Ethan had talked about her, I'd assumed she was a shifter. But no, she definitely was human, and she was going to break.

I leaped over to her and wrapped an arm around her shoulders. "It's okay, Mary Carol," I said. "Everything's going to be fine."

She tilted her head up and stared at me through glassy eyes. "How do you know my real name?"

"I met Ethan today," I said with a soft smile. "He was worried about you."

"Ethan," she choked out. Tears filled her eyes and spilled down her cheeks as her body shook with racking sobs.

I held her as I watched Allcot and his people annihilate the shifter pack. One after another, they all fell, everyone except Strix.

I spotted him slinking off in the shadows near where Iris was huddled with Leo. She was tending to his wounds, oblivious to what was going on around her.

"Dax!" I shouted, spotting him only a few feet away, dusting off after a particularly nasty brawl in the dirt.

His head turned in my direction.

"Behind you!"

He spun and came face-to-face with Strix. The vampire gave Dax a slow grin, then nodded as if accepting a challenge. Dax did the same. The pair circled each other, and I wanted to scream in frustration. This wasn't a fucking match in a ring, it was an all-out war. Strix and his gang had tried to poison a large portion of the New Orleans shifter population. Thankfully, as far as we knew, they hadn't been as successful as they'd intended, but they'd still caused a lot of damage and left a lot of carnage in their wake. All I wanted was for someone to put them out of their misery.

But Dax wanted his blood. I could see it in his eyes. And Strix was welcoming him. Waiting for him to pounce.

"Someone needs to stop him," Mary Carol said.

"Stop who?" I asked her.

"Strix," she said, his name getting caught on a sob as she

pointed. "He... he has a gun." Light from the orange moon reflected off the silver barrel just as the words left her mouth.

"No!" I cried and launched myself in their direction, my magic spinning out of control as I tried to create some sort of shield to protect Dax. I felt more than heard the gun go off, then I was on the ground, my body cold and my breathing labored.

"Phoebe!" Dax hovered over me, his face tight with pure emotion. "Hold on. Just hold on. I've got you."

Dax? I tried to say, but no words came out. I couldn't feel my hands or my feet. Then my face went numb. *I'm dying. This is what it feels like to die,* I thought. *It's not so bad. No pain. No sense of trauma. Just nothing.*

But then Pandora was there. "Move!" She reached down and picked me up. My insides felt like they were being ripped to shreds as molten lava seared my gut. "Stay alive, Phoebe," she ordered. "Just stay alive."

I stared up at her perfect face, wondering if she was an angel. She had to be. No one was that beautiful.

Black crowded the edge of my vision, and I felt myself falling into the sweet abyss where nothing hurt and all I could see was a bright warm light. I didn't know how long I stood there, basking in the glow. Minutes? Hours? Days? There was no way to tell. It called to me, whispered my name. I reached for it, wanted it, and took a step forward. Peace settled around me. This was my destiny, where I was always supposed to end up.

"Phoebe!" Willow's angry voice interrupted my peaceful walk to the light.

"What?" I whined.

"Phoebe?" Her voice was full of awe and excitement now.

"Oh my goddess. Wake up, love. Open your pretty black eyes."

My lids fluttered and the bright light stung, making me turn my head, trying to hide from the light. "Why does it hurt? It didn't hurt before."

"Phoebs," Willow said gently. "You were shot in the stomach. You're in Imogen's clinic."

Imogen... The name meant something. My lids flew open and I tried to push myself up, only to grunt with pain as I lay back down. "Imogen? Where...?"

"I'm right here," she said, smiling down at me. "Welcome back. How are you feeling?"

"The antidote... Did you find one?"

She let out a chuckle and nodded. "Yes, Agent Kilsen. We did in fact find an antidote. Eadric ordered his factory to put it into production so that it's readily available should the need arise."

"Did everyone get it who needs it?" I asked.

"Mostly," she said with an air of mystery. "But don't worry about that now. You just need to take care of you. We've got the rest."

"Mostly? What does that mean?"

Willow appeared beside me again, this time shaking her head at Imogen. "I told you she'd want the information as soon as she woke up. You might as well just tell her."

I glanced over at my friend. Her red hair was pulled back into a low ponytail. That was a sure sign she hadn't showered in at least a few days. And there were dark shadows under her blue eyes. "Wil?"

"Yeah?"

"How long have I been in here?"

She squeezed my hand. "Four days."

"Whoa." I closed my eyes again, this time trying to take stock of what my body was telling me. Everything ached. My head, my back, my gut, even my toes. But I was alive thanks to Pandora and Imogen, and no doubt Willow and Tal. "It feels like I was only out for a few minutes."

"It happens like that sometimes," Imogen said as she adjusted something on the med machine.

"Are you giving me drugs? Am I going to get loopy here in a minute?" I asked her.

She shook her head. "Not until you tell me you need them."

I eyed her suspiciously. "Seriously?"

She laughed. "Seriously. But if you overdo it, I'll stop taking your wishes into consideration."

"Fair enough."

She made a note in my chart. "There are a few people waiting to see you. Are you ready for more visitors?"

"Dax," I said without even thinking about it.

"He'll be here in a few hours," Willow said. "But Leo and Iris are here."

"Okay," I said with a yawn, feeling the exhaustion settle in my bones.

"Five minutes," Imogen said and then opened the door.

The pair walked in, all smiles and bright with youth. "Hey, you two." I mustered up some enthusiasm. "You doing okay?"

Iris clasped her hand in mine and squeezed. "We're doing just fine. It's you we're worried about."

I lifted my hand and made a gesture intended to wave away their concerns. "I'm fine. It's not the first time I've been wounded on the job. God knows I have the scars to prove it."

They shared a glance, then Leo turned to Willow. "You haven't told her what happened?"

"Not yet. I was waiting until someone who was there could relay the story."

My eyes popped open. "What happened? Is everyone all right? Dax? Pandora and Allcot? What about the shifters who were infected with the toxin? Are they okay?"

Leo laughed. "Whoa, slow down there, Agent. Yes, everyone is fine. The antidote Talisen and Imogen came up with has cleared the toxin from all the shifters the Void was holding. The ones who survived the brawl at Strix's house have also been treated."

"The ones who survived... Who perished?" I asked.

"King and Boomer," Leo said.

I didn't know who Boomer was, but I'd been standing right there when Mary Carol landed the death blow to King, so that wasn't a surprise. "Mary Carol, is she getting help?"

Iris nodded. "Allcot set her up with a therapist."

"Well... that was kind of him," I said dryly.

"He seemed most grateful."

"I bet." My head was starting to swim, but I had to know. "Is it over? Is the toxin off the streets?"

"Yes, Phoebs, it's over," Leo said solemnly, then proceeded to fill me in on everything they'd learned from King about Paul Macer and his desire to take on Cryrique. "It turns out that the billionaire stumbled on the toxic substance while trying to re-create Scarlet. He employed King to get the project off the ground over here. King partnered with TR who was skimming Scarlet off legitimate orders and making bank by selling it to King and Strix and other small-time dealers."

"I assume Allcot took care of him," I said.

"You have to ask?" I heard Willow say in the background.

"Just making sure," I shot back.

She chuckled. "You wouldn't be you if you didn't."

Leo and Iris spent a few more minutes visiting until Imogen shooed them out. "Time for rest," she said and hit a button on my drug machine. The sweet pain reliever kicked in, and in moments I was out, dead to the world in a deep, dark sleep.

Chapter Twenty-Four

J'd been at Imogen's clinic for two more days and still hadn't seen Dax. I'd been told he'd been in and out the entire time, but I was always asleep when he was by my side. The signs were there. He'd left folders from my inbox, flowers, a card, and even some fresh-baked, nonmagical cookies after he heard I'd been complaining about the ones Willow was force-feeding me to get my strength up. She meant well, it was just that I was tired of raisins, and those were a main ingredient in her Oat-Mend cookies. I was done.

I sat up in bed and flipped the top file open. It was a report from IT on Hailee's phone. Everything I'd ever needed was in there. King's phone number, Macer's direct line, Strix's actual bayou address. How'd she get all that information? I flipped the page and found pictures of her on a yacht in a teeny-tiny bikini. She had one arm around King and the other around an older man I didn't recognize. He had his hand on her ass and was leaning in, kissing her neck.

I turned the photo over and learned the man in the picture was Macer.

There was an entire stack of pictures devoted to Hailee's attempts to woo the billionaire. Maybe she hadn't been the innocent college girl I'd pegged her to be. I slammed the folder shut. It wouldn't do anyone any good now. This morning we'd learned Hailee had perished after spending two days trying to recover from wounds incurred in the brawl outside's Strix's house. I couldn't say I was upset about it. She'd been attacked by one of the vampires while trying to choke the life out of Iris, so it wasn't as if she was blameless. But it was still hard to swallow.

The door swung open, and finally there was Dax.

He paused near the door and grinned at me. "You're finally awake."

"You look different."

He nervously ran a hand over his thick hair and glanced down at his jean-clad body. "How so?"

"Your hair is darker. Thicker too, I think. And did you shave this morning?"

He nodded.

"Your five-o'clock shadow is coming in about six hours too early." I scanned him from head to toe, and honestly, it wasn't that I didn't like what I saw. Because damn, he was looking fine as hell. It was just that it had been less than a week since I'd last seen him and suddenly he was resembling someone from a magazine cover. The dude was just hot. "Have you been working out and I just didn't notice? I mean, look at those arms."

He ran his hands over his forearms and closed his eyes as he seemed to gather himself. "Phoebs, there's something you need to know."

"Your voice is even deeper," I said. "How is that—?"

"Phoebe." He cut me off as I marveled at his appearance. "I'm trying to tell you something important."

"Okay." I sat up straighter and waited. "Shoot."

He moved to sit on the edge of my bed. Then he took my hand in his large one. "The antidote didn't seem to work on me."

I blinked twice. "What?"

"You know, Tal and Imogen's antidote… it didn't knock out all the toxins in my bloodstream."

"Okay." I cleared my throat, trying not to let panic set in. "What does that mean exactly?"

"Well, I'm not going to go crazy if that's what you're asking," he said with a soft smile.

I tightened my grip on his hand. "That's something at least."

"Yeah." He let out a humorless chuckle. "But the toxin is the reason for all these changes."

My eyebrows shot up. "That's not… I thought the toxin was to make stronger, better, more ruthless soldiers."

"It was, but the drug also enhanced other physical characteristics such as muscle tone and sometimes other random features such as hair and voice. Others are reporting growing a few inches or eye-color change." He shrugged. "But the common denominator is muscle mass. Macer really was building an army, and a lucky few of us are stuck with the side effects."

I raised one eyebrow. "If you have to be stuck with side effects, I can think of worse ones."

He laughed. "True. But it's disorienting when you're used to seeing one person in the mirror and suddenly you're something else."

"Poor guy," I said, only half teasing. "Do you want me to pretend I don't notice your sexy arms or this thick hair that I want to run my hands through?"

"No," he said, his voice suddenly husky. "Not at all."

"Good, 'cause when I get out of here, I can't wait to get my hands on you."

Dax cupped my cheek, leaned down, and brushed his lips over mine. "Promise me that when I take you home, you'll take it easy for a while."

"You're taking me to my home?" I asked. "What about yours?"

He shook his head. "I see how you dodged answering that."

I just smiled up at him. "What can I say? I'm a Void agent."

"Yeah, so I've heard." His eyes turned serious as he gazed down at me, brushing his fingertips over my jawline. "I haven't said thank you yet."

"For what?

"Saving my life. Don't think I forgot that you literally took a bullet for me."

"I wouldn't exactly put it that way," I said. "I mean, I would. You know I would. I just, I saw the gun and tried to shield you with my magic, but I guess Strix had been meaning to aim for me the whole time."

He leaned up on one elbow and shook his head. "No, Phoebs. You did shield me, but not only that, you directed the bullet to go toward you and not anyone else. You took that bullet for all of us."

"I did?" I asked, completely shocked. "I didn't... I mean, I had no idea."

"Get used to it, Kilsen. You're a fucking hero."

~

HERO OR NOT, I still had a job to do. After seven days in the infirmary, I was released from Imogen's care. By then everyone had gotten back to their regular lives, and I'd told Dax not to worry about picking me up. After he'd retrieved my car from the bayou, he'd left it in Imogen's parking lot for when I needed it.

Today I was finally going to make my way out to River Road. I hadn't forgotten about the tip Dax had received regarding my brother. And I'd had days lying in my room thinking about it. But I had a stop to make first.

The day was cooler than usual, the skies overcast and thick with the threat of rain. I loved it. The gloomy skies suited my mood perfectly. And if it rained, all the better. It would be like a cleansing to wash away all that had happened in the past few weeks.

The first drops started to fall just as I pulled into Simone's driveway. Her small Caribbean-blue cottage was so happy looking set against the dark green of the bayou. I'd been told she'd woken with no memory of the attack or why she'd been in the library in the first place. I wanted to find out if that was true.

Armed with her notebook I'd found in the library the day after the attack, I stepped out of my car and made my way up her walk. Before I even made it onto her front porch, Simone opened the door and leaned in the doorway. Her dark curls were tied up with a brightly colored yellow-and-blue scarf, and she wore a matching sundress that complemented her dark skin.

"It's about time you came to see me," she said, her heavy

Cajun accent making me smile as she waved me in. "I heard you had a couple of exciting weeks."

"Just about as exciting as yours, only I remember what happened to me," I said, stepping inside her air-conditioned home.

Her smile vanished. "They told you I didn't remember?"

"Yes. Is that not true?"

She shook her head, then took me by the hand and led me to her small kitchen table. Two glasses had already been filled with iced tea. "Sit." She gestured to one of the glasses. "Drink up. I made it special for this visit."

I did as I was told, then eyed her. "How did you know I was coming today?"

She just shrugged. "Swamp witches, we know these things."

"Fair enough." I placed her notebook on the table. "Want to tell me what happened that night?"

"There's not much to tell. I was in the library waiting for you when Allcot's vampire showed up."

"Tanner?" I asked.

"No. His name is TR. I'd met him once before at a Cryrique benefit." Her dark eyes narrowed with the memory. "He was very average: average height, light brown hair, dull brown eyes. He'd have been very forgetful if he hadn't been leering at me and drooling on my cleavage."

I grimaced. "Jeez. It's always the harmless-looking ones that are the worst."

"Always," she agreed with a shake of her head. "First he tried flirting with me and wanted to give me a taste of that shit he sells. What do they call it? Scarlet?"

"Yeah. He really tried to get you to try it?" Simone wasn't even a shifter. What was he trying to do, kill her? The answer was obvious. If he was offering a witch Scarlet, there was no other explanation.

"Yes. In fact, he wasn't taking no for an answer. Finally I told him I wasn't interested then grabbed it out of his hand and broke the needle. No one needs that crap. It kills."

At least that explained why there had been a green syringe in her hand. TR, we'd learned, had also been Strix's supplier. He'd been distributing the tainted drug as well as some that was pure to his regular clients. "Then what happened?"

"The son of a bitch lost his mind and attacked me. Told me to keep my trap shut, that no one was to know about the portals. Said Allcot sent him."

Allcot, that piece of work. Had he really sent TR to kill Simone or just to stop her from sharing her information. If so, why? What did he care if I learned about some hypothetical portals? "Did he give you any clues as to why Allcot sent him?"

She shook her head. "No idea. The information I was trying to share with you is ancient magic, an area I'm interested in studying. I thought maybe we could look into it together." She tapped the notebook I'd brought back to her. "Were you able to take a look at this?"

I let out a small chuckle. "Look at it, yes. Translate it, no. I was a little busy."

"I figured that's what you'd say." She took a long sip of her iced tea, then flipped the book open. "See this?" She pointed to a small drawing that resembled an open door.

"Yeah."

"It's called the Window to the Other. It's a portal to a parallel universe."

"And what does that mean?" I studied the picture and the

girl who stood in the middle of the portal with one foot in one universe and one in another. The half of her body that was in the second universe was hidden from the viewer.

"It means we all have two lives. One in this world and another in an alternate universe that depicts our lives had we made different choices at pivotal moments."

I blinked a few times, trying to process what she'd just said. "Two paths, that's what you're saying?"

"Yes. And if we can open a window to another universe, would we want to? Should we? Would the temptation to see our lives in another light be too great for us? If we knew this existed, would we be able to resist?"

"I don't have the answers to those questions."

She shrugged. "Neither do I. But I find them fascinating. And now I want to know why Eadric Allcot wants to keep me from even asking them."

"So do I," I said, once again finding myself conflicted about the man who'd just helped save my life and the lives of my loved ones. How could he order an attack on a harmless —well, seemingly pleasant—swamp witch one day and then step up the moment I called asking for help? Of course, I had asked Pandora for help, and when it came to Pandora, everyone knew she was Allcot's weakness. He'd do anything for her, just like I'd do anything for Dax.

"There's a lot going on behind those dark eyes of yours, Agent Kilsen."

"Just inner turmoil," I said, shaking my head. "I know you're supposed to believe people when they show you who they are the first time. My problem is that some of them keep showing me radically different versions."

She tilted her head to the side and studied me. "But are they really showing you different people?"

Were they? I wasn't sure.

"Just think about it," she said.

"I will."

"Good. Now, is there anything else I can help you with today?" She was already standing up, and I took that as my cue to stand as well.

"Yes. Do you think these portals are real?"

She shrugged. "It doesn't matter what I think, it only matters what is real."

I sucked in a breath and tried not to say something stupid or refer to her as Yoda. Instead, I asked, "Have you seen one?"

"No. But I believe you may have."

She was referring to the area across the street from the Greek revival-style Creole townhome I shared with Willow. Six weeks ago, my brother had come back into my life after being missing for eight years with no explanation. Then he'd disappeared into thin air right before my eyes. I hadn't seen a window or any portal though. Seth had simply been there one minute and gone the next. "I'm not so sure," I said. "I'm not going to say it's impossible, but it doesn't feel probable, or at least it didn't until I learned Allcot doesn't want this information out."

"It's interesting how when someone is desperate to keep something secret, their goal becomes nearly impossible, don't you think?"

I couldn't help but agree.

Chapter Twenty-Five

The skies had opened up and drenched southeastern Louisiana while I'd been having iced tea with the swamp witch. We'd discussed the possibilities of a portal, or some sort of earthbound wormhole or even an opening to another dimension here on earth, like heaven or hell or something in between.

Simone was still speculating that Seth was living in another parallel universe. I was half convinced I'd dreamed the entire thing. I'd have stuck with that if my brother hadn't actually been there when we'd fought a sorceress who'd been planning to suck the life out of my best friend. None of that had been an illusion. I had the scars to prove it.

By the time I left, I was just as confused as ever and was dying to call Allcot on his bullshit... again. The idea of him ordering one of his shady vamps to attack Simone made my stomach turn. One of these days, I was going to learn there was no honor buried deep inside that arrogant vampire. No matter how many good deeds he racked up, he was still an opportunistic bully who didn't deserve my trust.

But instead of turning my car back toward the city, I pointed it toward River Road. That tip that Dax heard about my brother would haunt me unless I checked to see for myself. Who knew? Maybe my wild-goose chase in regard to portals and magical windows would prove to be utter nonsense. Maybe my brother really was living on an old plantation, and for whatever reason he felt like he couldn't get in touch.

If that was the case, I was going to remedy that fear today.

The sun started to peek out from behind the clouds just as I reached River Road. I made a left turn and headed west, keeping my eyes peeled. Most of the restored plantations had already been turned into tourist spots. A few appeared to be deserted, but a handful were definitely lived in. I stopped by two. At the first one I chatted with a stay-at-home dad. At the second one I spoke with a house manager. Neither had seen or heard of my brother, but both admitted that because the plantations aren't all that close to each other, they didn't interact with their neighbors as much as they'd like. If Seth was new to the area, they probably hadn't met him yet.

I thanked them both for their time and continued on. After three more stops and three more misses, I was ready to turn around and head back to New Orleans. That was my intention when I pulled into the circular driveway of a run-down plantation. But before I could turn around, I spotted a little boy with brown hair, brilliant blue eyes, and a lanky body that was the spitting image of Seth when we'd been kids.

My foot hit the brake, and my car came to an abrupt stop as I watched the little boy run across the yard toward me, calling for his dad.

"Daddy, Daddy, who's that?"

The kid pointed right at me. Somehow I'd managed to get out of my car and was standing in front of the kid, staring at him in awe. The resemblance was uncanny.

"Phoebe?" Seth's voice penetrated my foggy brain. "What the hell are you doing here?"

"I…" I cleared my throat and moved toward him, letting my anger fortify me. "I came looking for you. I think the real question is what the hell are *you* doing here? Can't you just pick up a phone and say, 'Hey Phoebs, I'm down here on River Road with my family. Don't worry, we're great, and visit soon.' Or is it the 'visit soon' part that gives you hives?"

"That's not—" He shook his head, dropped the ball he was holding, and placed both hands on my shoulders as he moved me backward. "You can't be here."

I dug my heels into the dirt. "Why not? Are you scared to introduce me to your son? It's obvious he's yours, you know. Or what? Will your wife not approve of a vampire hunter? I'm not here for money. I can take care of myself, you know. All I want to know is that you're okay and have a little glimpse into your life. What's wrong with that?"

"That's what's wrong with that." He spun me around and pointed at a woman who was dressed in a peach-colored cotton dress with white polka dots and flip-flops who, despite the unfortunate fashion choices, could've been my doppelgänger.

"Sweet Jesus, please don't tell me that woman is your wife. Is that why you don't want me around?"

"Oh for God's sake. No, that isn't it." He mock-gagged and then whispered in my ear. "She's you, you idiot. Now get the hell out of here before she figures out there's an opening."

"An opening, what?" I said stupidly then watched as my

twin's, my doppelgänger's, eyes widened right before she sent me a cold, calculating smile, then disappeared into thin air.

I spun, searching for Seth, and let out a huge sigh of relief when I spotted him still standing behind me. "Thank you, Jesus. How do people keep doing that? I don't understand. Simone thinks there are portals to alternate universes, but I'm more inclined to believe different dimensions. I mean, how can there be two of each of us living entirely different but parallel lives at the same time?"

Seth pressed a hand to his forehead and said, "Lex, please go tell your mommy that Aunt Phoebe needs a fresh change of clothes."

"Sure, Daddy." The little boy jumped up and planted a kiss on Seth's cheek, making my heart melt into a mushy puddle of goo.

I watched as he ran into the house that wasn't nearly as dilapidated as I'd first thought. The siding appeared to be new and freshly painted. The roof was in good shape, but the columns needed some work. So did the windows on the south side. But other than that, it was gorgeous.

Frustration coiled up and made me want to lash out, but I held it back, not wanting to get into a full-blown fight just minutes after finding him again. I turned and held Seth's gaze as I said, "Please don't push me away. Whatever it is, can we just try to work through it? I don't want to keep missing out on moments in your life. This house, your boy, both are amazing. And I don't even know who you're married to."

"Seth?" A tall blonde floated out of the house. "Your sister's dress is hanging in the laundry room."

My mouth fell open as I took in her curves and the strong

cheekbones. Was that… Holy hell. It was. It had to be. *Pandora*, only she was in human form.

"Phoebe, what in the world are you wearing?" Pandora asked, shaking her head.

I could've said the exact same thing about her outfit. She was wearing shorts. Shorts, of all things, and a tank top. I'd never seen Pandora so dressed down in her life. Not unless she was in her fancy lingerie while she strutted around for Allcot. Only I refrained from mentioning anything about her clothing, because I wasn't rude. I glanced down at my ripped jeans, work boots, and T-shirt that said STAKE IT LIKE A GIRL. "Clothes?"

"Just don't let Eadric see you in that. You know how he feels about those 'designer' jeans," she said.

I turned to Seth. "Why should I give a fuck what Eadric thinks of my clothes?"

He let out a long sigh. "Remember what you were saying about your friend thinking there were parallel universes?"

"Yeah."

"Well, she's right." He waved a hand at the house and Pandora, who was already disappearing back inside. "And you just stepped into one."

"But—" I glanced around, noting my car was gone. It too had somehow vanished into thin air.

"And the girl in the polka-dot dress? That was you who lives in this universe. She just took over your life in the world you know. Now you're stuck here until she decides to come back."

I stared at him, thunderstruck. "What?"

"Parallel universe, Phoebe. You just told me how you already know all about it. Well, congratulations, you found one." He sounded panicked and out of control, not at all like the brother I'd grown up with.

"Seth?" I asked, hearing the trepidation in my own voice.

"Yes?"

"What happened in the second grade that gave me this scar?" I pointed to the jagged, rough patch of skin on my elbow.

He studied my arm for just a moment, frowning. Then a grin split his lips as he let out a laugh. "Danny Freeman stabbed you with a pencil after you called him out for picking his nose."

"Oh, thank God!" I threw my arms around him and gave him a giant hug. "You're you. Not some strange version of you."

"Yeah, about that——"

"Phoebe?" A man who looked to be in his midtwenties stepped out onto the porch. "There you are." He had blond hair, piercing gray eyes, and… was a vampire. A daywalking vampire. I could tell by his smooth, familiar movements. He moved with grace and had that ethereal look vampires always had. He strode right up to me, and immediately I was on guard, wishing I'd thought to strap my new dagger to my boot.

"You found me," I said, still tense and on guard.

He smiled at me, a familiar cat-that-ate-the-canary smile that I'd seen at least a hundred times over the years. A smile that belonged to Eadric Allcot. Was this version a relative?

"I've got something for you," he said.

I raised my eyebrows in question. "What is it? Another *Little House on the Prairie* dress?"

His gaze swept over me, and he frowned when he took in my jeans. "It'd be better than those. Now will you please go change before our guests arrive? They'll be here in less than ten minutes."

Before I could even respond, he bent down and dropped a sweet, lingering kiss on my lips. I was so shocked I didn't even move until he was already back in the house.

I turned back to Seth. "Please tell me that isn't who I think it is."

"Do you want me to lie?"

I shook my head.

"I didn't think so," Seth said. "Get used to it, little sister. In this world, you're married to the vampire Eadric Allcot."

I let out a gasp and covered my mouth as I whispered, "Married?"

"Married. But look on the bright side, at least you don't have to sleep with a teenager. This version was turned the day after he turned twenty-six." Seth locked his arm through mine and practically dragged me across the yard.

Just before we got to the deck, I whispered, "Do I have kids?"

He shook his head. "Not yet."

"Yet?" I said with a gasp. "Does that mean I'm trying?"

"Eadric thinks so." He gave me a sympathetic smile. "Sorry, Phoebs. I tried to warn you."

I stared at him, my eyes wider than a deer's in headlights. Then I said the only words that popped into my mind. "But he's a vampire."

"Welcome to the twilight zone," he said. "Buckle up, because your life is about to get really interesting."

Deanna's Book List

Pyper Rayne Novels:
Spirits, Stilettos, and a Silver Bustier
Spirits, Rock Stars, and a Midnight Chocolate Bar
Spirits, Beignets, and a Bayou Biker Gang
Spirits, Diamonds, and a Drive-thru Daiquiri Stand

Jade Calhoun Novels:
Haunted on Bourbon Street
Witches of Bourbon Street
Demons of Bourbon Street
Angels of Bourbon Street
Shadows of Bourbon Street
Incubus of Bourbon Street
Bewitched on Bourbon Street
Hexed on Bourbon Street

Last Witch Standing Novels:
Soulless At Sunset
Bloodlust By Midnight

Bitten At Daybreak

Crescent City Fae Novels:
Influential Magic
Irresistible Magic
Intoxicating Magic

Witches of Keating Hollow Novels:
Soul of the Witch
Heart of the Witch
Spirit of the Witch

Witch Island Brides:
The Vampire's Last Dance
The Wolf's New Year Bride
The Warlock's Enchanted Kiss
The Shifter's First Bite

Destiny Novels:
Defining Destiny
Accepting Fate

About the Author

New York Times and USA Today bestselling author, Deanna Chase, is a native Californian, transplanted to the slower paced lifestyle of southeastern Louisiana. When she isn't writing, she is often goofing off with her husband in New Orleans or playing with her two shih tzu dogs. For more information and updates on newest releases visit her website at deannachase.com.

Made in the USA
Columbia, SC
22 May 2019